D0013080

The Case of the
Not-So-Nice Nurse

She kissed the girl back with all her might.

A Nancy Clue Mystery

The Case of the
Not-So-Nice Nurse

by Mabel Maney

CLEIS
PRESS

For Tom Metz, the real Cherry Aimless.

Thanks to Gigi Hanna for the title.

Copyright ©1993 by Mabel Maney.

Published in the United States by Cleis Press Inc., P.O. Box 8933, Pittsburgh, Pennsylvania 15221, and P.O. Box 14684, San Francisco, California 94114

Cover and interior design: Peter Ivey
Cover painting: Lesley Ruda
Frontispiece: Susan Synarski
Cleis logo art: Juana Alicia

FIRST EDITION
10 9 8 7 6 5 4
Printed in the United States of America

Library of Congress Cataloging-in-Publication Data
Maney, Mabel, 1958–
    The case of the not-so-nice nurse / Mabel Maney.
    -- 1st ed.   p. cm.
    ISBN 0-939416-75-1 (cloth) : $24.95. --
    ISBN 0-939416-76-X (paper) : $9.95
        1. Lesbians--United States--Fiction. 2. Girls--United
States--Fiction. I. Title.
PS3563.A466C37 1993
813'.54--dc20   93-11846
                                                      CIP

Contents

CHAPTER 1

A Tragic Blunder

Cherry Aimless cut an attractive figure as she dashed through the crowded lobby of Seattle General Hospital, her striking royal blue nurse's cape sailing behind her and her crisp white cap perched precariously on rumpled curls. Her rosy cheeks were even more flushed than usual, for she had run the entire ten blocks from the children's free clinic so as not to be late for the night shift on the Women's Psychiatric Ward. On clinic days the head nurse usually forgave a late entrance, but there would be no forgiving smile awaiting her now, for Head Nurse Margaret Marstad, the strictest nurse in the hospital, would be Cherry's boss tonight.

Cherry was in a cheery mood, for tomorrow morning she would begin a well-deserved vacation. "In just a few days I'll be in sunny San Francisco!" she murmured happily. While she was certainly looking forward to visiting her family in Pleasantville, Idaho, for a few days first, she had to admit she was more excited about going to San Francisco to see her beloved Aunt Gertrude. Although they had kept up a regular correspondence for the past five years, the two hadn't seen each other since Cherry was a child. "And I haven't had a chance to thank her properly for this nifty graduation present," Cherry thought, looking fondly at the sturdy nurse's watch Aunt Gert had sent her when she graduated from Stencer Nursing School, class of 1957.

"Jeepers!" she cried, realizing the time. "In another minute, I'll be late!" Cherry took a shortcut through the hospital newsstand, and in her haste caught the toe of her freshly-polished white nurse's shoe on a crack in the linoleum floor. She landed face first on a bundle of newspapers.

ATTORNEY CARSON CLUE MURDERED!
Longtime housekeeper admits dastardly deed!

screamed the headline.

"I'll take a paper!" she cried, searching in the pocket of her white uniform for a dime.

"I'm sorry miss, I have to count the papers before selling any," the newsstand operator explained. The frantic look on Cherry's face convinced him to hurry, and soon she was racing toward the elevator grasping a copy of the *Seattle Post*. For once Cherry was thankful that the creaky old elevator was its usual slow self, for it gave her a chance to read.

> River Depths, Illinois—*Well-known attorney Carson Clue was found shot through the heart early today in the kitchen of his exclusive River Depths home. Although he was a successful attorney in his own right, Carson Clue was perhaps best known as the father of girl detective Nancy Clue, whose exploits are familiar to newspaper readers everywhere.*
>
> *In a dramatic call to police, long-time housekeeper Hannah Gruel confessed that she had murdered the popular attorney during a domestic quarrel.*
>
> *"I told that man time and time again to keep out of my kitchen while I was baking!" Miss Gruel declared as she was led away in handcuffs to the Illinois State Prison for Women.*
>
> *According to Miss Gruel, at the time of the shooting, Nancy Clue was camping with her closest chums Bess Marvel and George Fey at nearby Lake Merrimen. After making a short statement to the police, the young detective headed west to stay with relatives.*

Cherry read the story over and over as the elevator crept to the sixth floor. She could scarcely believe it—Nancy Clue's father dead at the hands of kindly housekeeper Hannah Gruel! It just couldn't be!

Why, just last night, while relaxing in the probation nurses' lounge, Cherry had read an article about the Clues and their beloved housekeeper Hannah. The latest issue of

Girls' Life magazine had arrived that day in a care package from her mother, along with dusting powder, cologne and iced raisin cookies. Her roommate, Nurse Cassie Case, a perky brunette with a winning smile, stopped by the lounge to sample one of Mrs. Aimless's prize-winning cookies. She kidded Cherry when she caught her carefully tearing a photo of Nancy from the magazine. "Is that for your shrine?" she joked.

Cherry had blushed. It was no secret that she practically worshipped Nancy Clue. More than anything, Cherry wanted to be courageous and forthright, like Nancy. Although they were as different as two girls could be, Nancy with her immaculately groomed titian hair, charm school education and fearless nose for danger, and Cherry, a small-town girl with a hopeless mop of unruly curls and a shy manner, she nonetheless felt that, given the right opportunity, they could become fast friends.

"Nancy's done so much good for so many; if only there was something I could do to help her!" she cried aloud, forgetting for a moment that she was in a crowded elevator. She clapped a hand over her mouth and blushed a deep crimson. Thankfully, the elevator had arrived at her floor. She tucked the newspaper under her arm and rushed from the crowded elevator—and smack into Head Nurse Margaret Marstad!

"Oh, I'm so sorry!" Cherry cried, reaching out a hand to help the handsome head nurse regain her balance. Nurse Marstad haughtily straightened her cap and got a grip on her armload of medical charts.

"Nurse Aimless, you're late," she said curtly as she stepped into the vacancy Cherry had left in the elevator. "And fix your cap; it's all askew," she added, as the doors closed in front of her frowning face. Cherry brushed aside hot tears and raced past the main nurse's station and down the long, brightly-lit corridor that led to the Women's Psychiatric Ward. She straightened her cap and raced through the oak double-doors opening onto the ward.

Nurse Penny Perkins was waiting for Cherry at the far end of the open thirty-bed ward. She smiled when she saw her frazzled friend.

"Am I ever glad to see you," said Penny. "I told Marstad that the clinic called and said there was an emergency and you would be late, but you know how strict she is. Why, the way she acts, we might as well be in the army!"

Cherry nodded. It was no secret that Nurse Marstad was a tough taskmaster. She was just about to tell Nurse Perkins about her run-in with Nurse Marstad, but her co-worker wasn't finished yet.

"It's been so quiet all day Marstad asked me to go help out in Emergency. Call her at her office if you need help," she added as she threw a regulation nurse's sweater over her strong shoulders and began gathering up her things.

Cherry shuddered at the thought of admitting to Nurse Marstad that she needed help. When Cherry had met the capable yet stern head nurse a year ago at her interview for the coveted job of General Hospital nurse, she had resolved to be the best probation nurse ever. More than anything, she wanted Nurse Marstad to like her!

"Now I'm in trouble because I stopped to get the evening paper," she thought, unfolding the newspaper she had tucked under her arm, intending to show the headline to Nurse Perkins. "Guess what happened!" she cried. But before she could continue, the emergency light flashed twice.

"That's my call," Nurse Perkins said gaily, sweeping past Cherry and heading toward the elevator. She waved back at Cherry. "I should be back in a couple of hours. Tell me then."

While Cherry was most anxious to discuss the murder of Carson Clue, she realized she had a job to do, and got on with the business of nursing. It was almost time for evening medications, and Cherry busied herself preparing the pills and injections that would help her patients get a good night's sleep. A half hour later her task was completed, and she found her attention wandering back to the newspaper story. Try as she might, she just couldn't stop thinking about the murder. Something just didn't seem right.

"Hannah's been like a mother to me," Nancy had been quoted in the *Girls' Life* article. "How strange," Cherry mused, "that helpful Hannah, who had given a lifetime of care to Mr. Clue and his motherless daughter, should turn out to be a murderess." She wished she had time to examine the newspaper article. Perhaps there was something she had missed, something that would explain the odd turn of events.

Like her heroine, Cherry had earned a reputation as a detective. In her first month at General Hospital she had solved the mystery of the vanishing valium. Using cool logic and keen sleuthing, she was able to follow a trail to Dr. Kildare and expose him as a thief who supported a lavish lifestyle by selling dangerous drugs pilfered from the hospital. Now her detective skills were being put to good use on the psychiatric ward, where hospital authorities had twice called upon her to help identify amnesia victims.

The drama of hospital life suited Cherry, who was happiest when she was helping others. The recent nursing school graduate found her work at the big city hospital exciting after a lifetime in the sleepy farm town of Pleasantville, Idaho. And she especially loved a good mystery! She had already helped to identify one amnesia victim, now home and safe with her family. But try as she might, she wasn't getting any closer to identifying the other amnesiac, tagged Jane Doe #313 by hospital authorities, but nicknamed Lana by the nurses because of her striking resemblance to the beautiful blond movie star Lana Turner.

There certainly weren't many clues to go on, Cherry thought as she reviewed the case. Lana had appeared at the hospital two days before, carrying a paper sack containing a small black plastic comb, a brand-new tube of red lipstick, and a hardcover book to which she seemed unnaturally attached. No identification papers were found, and her simple, well-made clothes had no labels.

Lovely Lana quickly became the newest attraction on the ward, charming everyone with her delightful manners and sweet disposition. Even gruff Head Nurse Marstad had succumbed to her charms and had been seen at Lana's bedside with a box of chocolates in her hand.

So far, Cherry had been frustrated in her attempts to draw anything personal out of Lana, who had remained vague during their two late-night conversations. Cherry sighed. Despite all her efforts, she had been unable to find even one piece of the puzzle.

"Tonight I'll try extra hard to dig up a clue," she vowed, as she carried the tray of medication through the ward. She smiled as she surveyed the attractive room, painted a cheery salmon and filled with flowers. Many nurses disliked the night shift, and would have let the long hours dampen their spirits, but not Cherry. She loved nursing under any conditions, and she especially liked working at the overcrowded old city hospital, where the patients really seemed to need her.

As a young girl she had often dreamt of a night just like tonight; dreamt of being in charge of a ward of patients, ready to soothe their pain using her gentle bedside manner in combination with the most up-to-date medical equipment available. Cherry patted her little cap and smoothed her hair into place. What a picture she made with her starched white uniform ironed just so and her crisp white cap pinned at a jaunty angle atop shiny black curls.

Suddenly the squeak of rubber-soled nurse's shoes on shiny linoleum woke Cherry from her daydream.

"Sleeping on the job, Nurse Aimless?" Nurse Marstad asked, her arched eyebrows framing steely gray eyes. Cherry was too afraid to answer. She shook so hard the pills on her tray rattled.

"Well, Nurse?" Nurse Marstad asked, tapping her pencil against the little black book she held in her hand. Everyone knew Nurse Marstad kept a record of every infraction and referred to the book when deciding upon promotions and salary increases. Cherry had worked and prayed all year for a promotion from probation nurse to permanent staff, and so far her record was spotless. But today she had been caught off her guard twice. Surely Nurse Marstad wouldn't be so cruel as to blemish her record over these slight transgressions? Or would she?

Cherry looked at the stern nurse through teary eyes. Nurse Marstad was scribbling furiously in her book. Hadn't her mother warned her to get her head out of the clouds before something terrible happened? "Oh, why didn't I listen to mother?" Cherry groaned to herself. "And on the eve of my big vacation!"

Cherry took a few deep calming breaths and got down to the business of nursing, under the austere gaze of Nurse Marstad. She was relieved to see that her first patient was Miss Lillian Bee, a quiet elderly woman suffering from a strange sleeping sickness. Cherry took a deep breath and began preparing Miss Bee's injection. She blushed as she readied the syringe. Nurse Marstad's attention made her nervous, and she clumsily dropped the needle. She hastily prepared a fresh injection, hoping the head nurse hadn't noticed.

But she *had* noticed and was making another notation in her black book. Cherry blushed a deep crimson, her red cheeks highlighting her fair coloring and sparkling green eyes. She bit her ruby lips as she prepared a sterile needle. Giving injections was difficult for her, as she hated to cause the slightest bit of pain to any living creature, even if it was for their own good.

Just as she was moistening a cotton pad with antiseptic, a voice called for Nurse Marstad over the intercom. With a brusk "Carry on, nurse," Nurse Marstad left the ward. Cherry breathed a deep sigh of relief.

With Nurse Marstad gone, Cherry competently injected Miss Bee, plumped her pillow and gave her a relaxing shoulder rub. She was glad the head nurse had been called away. Cherry was an efficient and kind nurse, as her patients would willingly testify, but there was something about Nurse Marstad that always unnerved her!

She finished soothing Miss Bee, and moved to her next patient. It was Lana, the amnesia victim. Although there was nothing physically wrong with Lana, Cherry was sorely tempted to massage her, too. Tonight her patient seemed unusually sad. She was sitting on the edge of her narrow hospital cot, clutching her book, with a faraway look in her eyes. It took her a moment to realize Cherry was at her side.

"I bet she's upset because it's been two whole days and we haven't made any progress on her case," Cherry guessed, vowing to double her efforts to identify Lana. Perhaps there was something she'd overlooked, she thought, surveying Lana with keen eyes.

"Perhaps there's a clue in the book?" Cherry wondered. She remembered that Nurse Marstad had admitted Lana to the ward. "She's so thorough, she surely would have checked," Cherry realized.

Suddenly an idea came to her. "Lana must be married— she's wearing a gold band. I wonder if anyone has looked inside her ring. If it's engraved, it will be our first clue. I must see that ring!"

"Oh, what a pretty ring," Cherry remarked, trying to keep her tone casual.

"Like it?" Lana asked, polishing it on her hospital-issue

cotton smock. Somehow even the cotton gown looked like a couture dress on lovely Lana. "My honey gave it to me," she said, looking wistful. Much to Cherry's delight, Lana seemed genuinely interested in showing off her ring.

"Oh, your hands are so tiny! I bet that ring wouldn't fit on my pinkie!" Cherry exclaimed, hoping to get her hands on it.

It worked. Lana took off her ring and handed it to Cherry. "Try it on; I bet your hands aren't as big as you think."

Cherry slipped the ring on her finger, then took it off. She pretended to admire its smooth surface as she looked for an inscription. She found what she was looking for.

"*From G.A. to C.M. with love, 5-2-49*" read the inscription in tiny cursive writing. For some reason, the thought of Lana being married upset her. What kind of man would this woman marry? She could see why any man would want to marry Lana, for she was not only pretty, she was charming, friendly and witty as well.

"Why, if I were a man, I'd marry her," Cherry thought, blushing furiously at the idea. She realized Lana was looking at her with a penetrating gaze that made Cherry feel all flustered.

"Why, it's as if she can read my mind," Cherry thought, feeling a flush race up her cheeks. She hurriedly handed back the ring and gave Lana a little paper cup containing two pink pills.

"Thank you for showing me your lovely ring," she said. "Perhaps when I finish dispensing medication we can have a little talk and maybe you'll remember something about your husband," Cherry said.

Lana laughed merrily at this suggestion, squeezed Cherry's hand, and said she'd be delighted to have a nice chat.

"I have a feeling I'll really get somewhere tonight," Cherry thought happily as she went about her tasks. "I'm sure in no time at all Lana will be home, safe and sound!"

She hummed happily as she resumed her rounds, and her cheerful mood seemed to lift the spirits of her patients. In addition to giving out pills, Cherry always took a moment at each woman's bedside to ask about her progress. She became so engrossed in one patient's tale that it was almost an hour before she finished.

When she returned to Lana's bedside, she was surprised to see a nun sitting on the edge of the bed.

14

"Why, Sister, I didn't see you come in!" Cherry exclaimed. The nun pulled her veil closer around her face and said nothing.

Cherry wasn't accustomed to seeing nuns visiting during the night shift, and if the truth be known, the quiet creatures in head-to-toe black always made her a little nervous. The nun spoke to Lana in a low, hushed voice; Cherry could tell she wanted privacy. But Lana seemed to welcome the intrusion, and cheerfully called Cherry to her side.

"Nurse Aimless, I have that book you loaned me," Lana said, reaching under her pillow. She held out the book she had been guarding so carefully the last few days, and smiled. There was a queer animated tone in her voice, one Cherry hadn't heard before. She seemed like an actress playing a part.

"You were right—it's a great book! Especially chapter fifteen. Oh, boy, I laughed so hard I cried!" Lana continued merrily.

Cherry stumbled for an answer. She hadn't loaned this book to Lana. Was she playing a trick, Cherry wondered, or was her amnesia getting worse? Cherry decided the best thing to do was to play along, and took the book from Lana.

"Thank you for returning it so promptly," Cherry said. "There are others waiting to read it. I'm glad you enjoyed it."

Something was very queer here. "I'd better contact Dr. Spreck immediately!" Cherry thought.

But before she had a chance to telephone the doctor, she heard a shout.

"Nurse! Nurse!" came a muffled cry from outside the ward. Why, it sounded like someone was calling for help! Cherry raced out of the room and in the direction of the shouts, but by the time she reached the end of the long corridor, all was quiet. Strangely quiet. A priest sat calmly at the duty nurse's desk, reading a tattered magazine. He smiled at Cherry as she caught her breath.

"Goodness, my child, where's the fire? You don't want to break a leg and end up a patient at your own hospital, do you?" he chuckled in an affable manner.

"I though I heard a cry for help!" she exclaimed.

"Nonsense, I didn't hear a thing," the priest responded.

"But, but," Cherry stammered, her rosy cheeks flushed, her heart beating a mile a minute.

"But what, dear?" he asked, squinting at Cherry through thick black-framed glasses.

Cherry looked around the quiet room. Obviously, nothing had happened. Feeling foolish, she blushed some more. "I've got to get more sleep; now I'm hearing things!" she said to no one in particular, for the priest had gone back to his magazine, and the corridor was deserted.

Cherry strode briskly back to the ward, knowing she had broken a strict hospital rule against leaving patients unattended. She pushed open the double doors to the ward and looked around. She was relieved to see her patients all tucked quietly in their beds.

Except for Lana, who was nowhere to be seen!

"Where is Lana?" Cherry asked, trying to control the alarm in her voice. But most of her patients were already fast asleep.

She looked at Lana's bed. The half-eaten pork chop and glass of milk abandoned on the pink cafeteria tray looked so forlorn. What had happened to Lana?

"I've failed in my duty as a nurse," Cherry thought. Nurses were forbidden to leave their wards at the understaffed city hospital, and that went double for the psychiatric ward.

"Where is Lana?" she repeated.

"She left with that nun," a sleepy patient yawned.

Cherry was relieved to find that Lana hadn't wandered away on her own. "Maybe they went to chapel," she mused aloud.

"Who went to chapel?" a stern voice from behind her demanded to know. Cherry whirled around and found herself face to face with Head Nurse Margaret Marstad. And she was not smiling!

"What's all the commotion in here?" she asked, hands on her shapely hips.

"When Cherry left the ward Lana went away with a nun," the patient repeated. "Come to think of it, she was an awfully tall nun," she added helpfully.

As soon as she heard this, Nurse Marstad strode briskly to the telephone at the end of the room and called security.

When she returned, Cherry tried to explain why she had left the ward, but before she could open her mouth, Nurse Marstad spotted the book in Cherry's hand.

"What's this, nurse?" she asked, crisply. In all the excitement, Cherry had forgotten about the book. She quickly explained about Lana's mix-up. "I fear her amnesia is worse, and now she's disappeared!"

Nurse Marstad glanced furtively at the book, cleared her throat, and looked Cherry straight in the eye. "I loaned her the book, Nurse Aimless. She simply forgot which nurse gave it to her," she said in a convincing tone. "There's no need to mention it to security when they arrive; they have enough to deal with. You will report to my office as soon as your replacement gets here." The head nurse took the book from Cherry and left.

Cherry was so confused. She was sure Lana had arrived with the book. "But Nurse Marstad would never lie about a thing like that. Oh, I must have imagined the book belonged to Lana the same way I imagined hearing a call for help!"

Cherry swallowed hard, fighting back tears. She knew she had made a major blunder which could threaten her chances of joining the staff permanently. "Why, I'll surely be fired if I admit to Nurse Marstad that I'm hearing things!"

Nurse Mildred Middy arrived a few minutes later to replace the despondent nurse. Cherry was relieved to see someone she knew, and it took all her willpower to keep from breaking down at the sight of her chum. The two had been fast friends since their first day at General Hospital, and they shared the same devotion to nursing and dread of Head Nurse Margaret Marstad.

"Don't let Marstad scare you, Cherry. Why, everyone knows you're one of the best nurses here," comforted Mildred. "We won't let her fire you. She just can't!"

Suddenly, the loudspeaker interrupted Nurse Middy's soothing consolations. "Nurse Aimless, report to my office immediately," Nurse Marstad's voice barked over the intercom.

Cherry said good-bye to her chum and to her patients, expressing the hope that she would see them soon. As she waited for the elevator that would take her to the third floor and the head nurse's office, she thought of the years of dreaming and hard work that had brought her this far. Could it be that it was all about to end?

CHAPTER 2

An Important Assignment

Cherry faced Nurse Marstad with a heavy heart. She tried to explain what had happened, but the harder she tried, the more muddled everything got, until finally she burst into tears.

"Oh, I'm so ashamed!" she cried, covering her face with her hands. Nurse Marstad pulled a lavender handkerchief from her pocket and gave it to the tearful girl.

"Blow your nose, nurse," Nurse Marstad commanded with a gentleness in her voice that Cherry hadn't heard before. Cherry hastily wiped her tear-stained face, took out her compact, brushed her shiny nose with a light dusting of powder and put on a hint of pink lipstick.

"Feeling better?" Nurse Marstad wanted to know. Cherry just nodded, too afraid to trust her voice.

Nurse Marstad took a seat behind her stately oak desk, which was piled high with paperwork and medical journals. She motioned for Cherry to take a seat in one of the turquoise naugahyde chairs facing the desk. Cherry squirmed in the slippery chair. Just a year ago, she had sat in this very spot, convincing Nurse Marstad that she was probation nurse material. And now she feared she had made a tragic blunder!

"I feel so awful that Lana is missing!" Cherry cried. "It's all my fault; I should never have left the ward. It's just that when I heard a call for help, I ran out without thinking, but no one was there. Well, no one except this priest and, well, I would just hate myself if anything happened to Lana because of me." Cherry's voice trailed off.

"I'm worried about Lana, too," Nurse Marstad admitted. "But I have reason to hope she'll soon be back where she belongs."

"I'll do anything to make this right," Cherry cried. "I won't go to San Francisco—I'll stay here and find Lana myself. I'm a pretty good detective; why, just tonight I found three clues as to her true identity!"

Nurse Marstad looked interested at the revelation of this information. "Really? What did you uncover?" she asked.

"I know that she's married, and her initials are C.M. And she must be Catholic; why else would she get a visit from a nun?"

"You're very observant, Cherry. That's a fine quality in a nurse." Nurse Marstad pulled her black book from her uniform pocket. Cherry bit her lip. Once she counted all the mistakes Cherry had made that day, she'd surely fire her!

"Let's see," Marstad said, flipping through the pages. "A— Aarnes...ah, here you are. Aimless, Cherry. Hired July 5, 1958, with highest recommendations from Nurse Shirley Stern, Stencer Nursing School, Clearwater Falls, Idaho."

Cherry was surprised to hear a good review from her old teacher. From the way she had always singled her out in class, Cherry had assumed Nurse Stern hadn't liked her one bit.

Nurse Marstad continued. "My reports indicate you are a thoughtful and efficient nurse. I was pleased tonight to see the nice manner in which you handled Miss Bee. All your patients give you high marks." Nurse Marstad closed her book. "Now, I hate to see a good nurse lost because of one blunder. You shouldn't have left the ward, Cherry, and my guess is that you'll never make that mistake again."

Cherry shook her head. "Never," she said solemnly. "I'll do anything to keep my job," Cherry added earnestly.

"Of course you'll keep your job." Nurse Marstad seemed amused.

"You mean you're not going to fire me? I can stay?" Cherry squeaked, her voice cracking with emotion.

"The other nurses would have my head if I let our most popular nurse go!" Nurse Marstad replied.

Cherry blushed. She had had no idea she was so well-liked. She just did her best to work hard, be cheerful and keep her uniform clean and starched.

The head nurse looked sternly at Cherry. "I know I'm hard on you nurses, but this is a difficult job. Our patients really need us; this isn't a fancy private hospital for spoiled rich people."

"That's why I'm here," Cherry said solemnly. Nurse

Marstad nodded. Cherry's dedication was apparent to all who worked with her.

"I meant what I said about canceling vacation plans to stay here and find Lana," Cherry repeated earnestly. "You saw how many clues I dug up tonight. I know I can do it! First I'll find Lana and then I'll find out who she is!"

Nurse Marstad shook her head. "While your dedication is laudable, we here at General Hospital don't believe in working our nurses to the bone. I really think you should take that vacation, Cherry. Besides, weren't you also going home to Idaho? Won't your mother be awfully disappointed?"

Cherry was amazed that Nurse Marstad knew so much about her plans. "I didn't tell her I was coming. I wanted it to be a surprise," Cherry said. "I'm sure I can find Lana. I'd feel so much better knowing that I didn't leave you in a jam."

Nurse Marstad looked thoughtful. "Actually, Cherry, you could do me a really big favor. I need to get a package to a friend of mine in Oregon—and soon. Are you staying long in Idaho?" When Cherry replied that she intended to visit her family for no more than a day on her way to San Francisco, Nurse Marstad continued.

"Since you're going in that direction, you could drop it off. It would just be a few miles out of your way. It's very important, and there aren't many people I'd trust with it. But I know I can count on you, Cherry."

"Even though I seem to be imagining things?" Cherry fretted.

Nurse Marstad laughed. "You're just overworked, Cherry. Why, you're a splendid probation nurse!"

That was high praise coming from the strict head nurse, Cherry thought. Her bosom swelled with pride. "Why, I'd be honored to deliver a package for you, Nurse Marstad. What is it?"

Nurse Marstad seemed flustered by Cherry's inquiry. She quickly regained her composure and answered, in a casual manner, "Oh, it's a special experimental medication, and it's very fragile. You'd need to watch it along the way; don't leave it in your car unattended. Take it with you wherever you go. It's very rare. When you get to Oregon, deliver it right to my friend's front door; hand it to her personally. I'll get a map to you before you leave in the morning," she said. "Are you willing to do it?"

"Of course!" Cherry cried. "You can count on me, Nurse Marstad. I'd never let you down! Why, you're not nearly as tough as everyone says!" she added.

Nurse Marstad chuckled. "You assumed I was going to fire you because you made one mistake. After all, doesn't everyone say I'm so tough that I practically eat probation nurses for breakfast?"

Cherry didn't know what to say. She always tried to be diplomatic. "Everyone knows you have high standards. And there was that one nurse..."

"So that awful rumor about Nurse Rita Rooney is still making the rounds!"

Cherry had indeed heard the rumor. Why, all probies heard it the first day on the job. Legend had it that a beginning nurse made a simple mistake during surgery, and Nurse Marstad reprimanded her so harshly she hung herself that very night. Her ghost haunted the first-year nurses' quarters during the full moon, the senior nurses said.

"You mean she didn't hang herself because of you?" Cherry blurted out before she could stop herself.

"Nurse Rooney is very much alive and well and living in Key West with Nurse Greta Green. I should know. I was her roommate until the day Nurse Green showed up."

Cherry's jaw dropped. "But why do they tell that terrible story?" she asked indignantly.

Nurse Marstad smiled widely, revealing a darling dimple in her left cheek. "Someone's idea of a joke, I guess!" she shrugged.

Cherry was astonished. Why, Nurse Marstad wasn't the big bad wolf everyone thought!

"It would be an honor to deliver your package, Nurse Marstad," Cherry said proudly.

Nurse Marstad unlocked the bottom drawer of her desk and took out a bundle the size of a clutch purse, wrapped in brown paper and tied securely with white string. Using her fountain pen, she addressed the package in bold handwriting before handing it to Cherry.

She walked Cherry to the door, handed her the precious parcel, and resumed her no-nonsense tone of voice.

"Nurse Aimless, I order you to go and pack!" she said, with a stern tone in her voice but a twinkle in her eye. "And Cherry," she added in a whisper, "Mum's the word about Nurse Rooney. That story keeps probies on their toes, and I kind of don't mind it myself!"

Cherry impulsively hugged the older woman. "I'll send you a postcard," she promised. She suddenly felt in high spirits.

Why, Nurse Marstad was human after all! And really quite attractive when she smiled, Cherry thought, as she headed back to her room to begin packing.

She was almost to the nurses' dorm when she realized she still had Nurse Marstad's lavender handkerchief clutched in her hand. "I'll wash and iron it tonight and return it in the morning," she promised herself. She jammed the handkerchief in her pocket, her thoughts turning to other things.

She hated to leave before Lana was found, but deep in her heart she knew Nurse Marstad was right. She could use a rest. And besides, now she had an important package to deliver!

"Two whole glorious weeks, and they're all mine!" she thought happily, a little skip in her walk. General Hospital could not have had a happier nurse than vacation-bound Cherry Aimless.

CHAPTER 3

The Journey Begins

The distinctive creak of rubber-soled shoes outside her door woke Cherry from a deep slumber. Being careful not to disturb her roommate, Nurse Cassie Case, Cherry slipped out of bed, donned her pink-flowered chenille robe and fuzzy slippers, and quietly opened her door.

"I must have been dreaming," she thought when she peeked out and discovered no one in the hallway. "That, or I'm a little jumpy after the events of last night! I may as well get an early start on my trip," she reasoned, but when she saw the soft glowing dial of her electric alarm clock, she changed her mind.

"Three in the morning and I'm thinking of getting up?" she yawned, jumping back into bed and snuggling under the warm covers.

She slept in fits and starts the rest of the night. Once she thought she heard someone jiggling her doorknob, but decided she was imagining things. Eventually she resumed her slumber, and when she awoke, Nurse Case was gone. On her neatly-made bed was a note for Cherry:

I didn't want to wake you because you'll need all your rest for the trip ahead. Have a gay time in San Francisco!

Cherry hopped out of bed, gave her face a good scrubbing in the little corner sink and put on the travel outfit she had selected before going to bed, a cornflower-blue madras skirt, simple white cotton blouse and comfortable flats.

"It's just the ticket for a comfy car trip," she declared, surveying herself in the full-length mirror. She double-checked the contents of her stylish white leather suitcase and matching cosmetics bag before latching them securely. Cherry wasn't sure what the styles were in San Francisco, so she had packed a wide variety of outfits, from play clothes to formal wear. She put Nurse Marstad's package in her purse and left her room.

After a delicious breakfast of soft-boiled eggs, melba toast and fruit cup in the hospital cafeteria, Cherry had two stops to make. The first was the payroll office, to receive her vacation pay. There was an envelope attached to her pay packet, addressed to her in Nurse Marstad's unmistakable handwriting. Inside was a map of Oregon, a crisp ten-dollar bill, and a note.

Cherry, I really appreciate this—you are a lifesaver!
Use the money for gasoline and a treat. I've marked the
map so you know where you're going.
Have a good time—that's an order.
Peg Marstad

Cherry remembered that Nurse Marstad's lavender handkerchief lay crumpled in the pocket of last night's uniform, which she had thrown hastily into her suitcase. Her friends laughed when she packed her uniforms for a vacation trip, but Cherry knew that a nurse could be called into action at any time, and she wanted to be appropriately attired if such an occasion should arise.

Besides, she wanted to show off the uniform to her chums in Pleasantville.

She had forgotten all about the handkerchief the night before during an impromptu party thrown together by her chums. Nurse Dina Darling, an Iowa farm girl with big brown eyes and a fetching smile, had filched some cheese and crackers from the cafeteria, and Nurse Polly Pluck, a tall brunette with an elfin grin and a dancer's graceful body, had produced a bottle of sparkling apple cider. "For special occasions," she said when she popped the cork. For these hard-working nurses, a vacation was a special occasion, indeed.

Cherry resolved that she would wash and iron the handkerchief at her mother's house and promptly mail it back to Nurse Marstad—or Peg, as she had begun calling her in her mind.

Her next stop was Women's Psychiatric to ask about Lana. Nurse Gerry George reported that Lana was still missing, but they were certain she would be found soon.

"Now, don't you worry about a thing," said Nurse George as she escorted an anxious Cherry to the elevator. "Marstad said if you came around to send you on your way," Nurse George laughed. "I guess she knows you pretty well, Cherry. First to volunteer and last to leave. You'd make a great army nurse! Now, get out of here and have some fun!" She gave Cherry a quick hug and playfully shoved her into the elevator.

Cherry felt drawn to the handsome woman with her warm manner and soft brown eyes. Nurse George was someone she would certainly like to get to know better. "I'll send her a postcard, too," she decided.

She walked briskly to the hospital garage where she stored her 1953 dark blue Buick. "It's not a very glamorous car," she thought, comparing it to the flashy red convertible with white leather seats parked in the next space.

"But it's sturdy and dependable, just like me." She smiled at her reflection in the car window and patted her dancing black curls into place.

She put her suitcase and cosmetics bag in the trunk, checking twice to make sure the lock was secure. "If you must leave home, at least leave in style," her mother had sighed when she gave her the luggage as a high school graduation present.

Cherry hopped into the car and put her purse containing Nurse Marstad's package on the passenger seat beside her. Cherry sighed and settled into her seat. The drive home to Idaho would take at least eight hours, and she was eager to be on her way.

She pulled her car into a nearby service station, and while the attendant filled her tank, Cherry checked to make sure she had her maps of Washington and Idaho. Although she knew the route by heart, it comforted her to know they were available if she ran into trouble. Although Cherry had an excellent sense of direction, she refused to go anywhere without a map.

She was engrossed in planning the first leg of her journey when a strange man wearing a fedora pulled low over his face reached into her car and snatched her purse!

Cherry screamed, and the startled man dropped her purse and ran. The attendant raced after him, but to no avail.

"He disappeared around that corner," she said apologetically, handing Cherry her purse. "Are you all right, miss? Do you want me to call the police?"

Although Cherry was frankly shaken, she didn't want to lose any time. She wasn't as worried about her purse as she was about Nurse Marstad's precious parcel. What if it had been stolen? "I'd have to change my name and move to another town," she though grimly. "I'd never be able to face Nurse Marstad and admit I let her down."

She paid for the gasoline, thanked the attendant for her help, rolled up her windows and locked her doors. "No one's getting this purse away from me again," Cherry vowed.

She drove with her eyes securely on the road ahead and her thoughts back at the busy hospital, her many nurse chums, and the now even more mysterious Lana. At times she wanted to turn back, and as the miles passed, taking her further and further from Seattle, she felt a sense of apprehension. Had she failed as a nurse? Nurse Marstad didn't seem to think so. Cherry replayed the hour of Lana's disappearance again and again in her mind.

If only she hadn't left the room! "But I thought someone needed me," she consoled herself.

Still, she had a nagging feeling that somehow there was something she had missed. She mulled over the two lengthy conversations she had had with Lana. Although Lana was friendly, she had a way of turning the conversation away from herself, and both times Cherry was surprised to find *herself* the focus of the conversation.

It had been Lana who had urged her to fly in the face of family disapproval and visit her Aunt Gertrude in San Francisco. Cherry had wanted to visit her beloved aunt many times, but each time she talked of going, it seemed some family emergency had come up. Or was it that her family just didn't like Aunt Gertrude? Cherry knew that couldn't be. Why, everyone loved the attractive, vivacious Miss Aimless!

The thought of seeing her aunt after all these years put Cherry in a better mood. Still, she would have felt even happier had she been able to solve the puzzle of the lovely Lana.

Cherry was proud of her sleuthing abilities. Hadn't she saved poor Miss Pringle's farm from being sold out from under her by her unscrupulous nephew? Cherry smiled as she remembered how, working as visiting nurse to Miss Polly Pringle of Pleasantville the summer after getting her R.N., she had uncovered the nephew's spiteful scheme and stopped the sale just in time.

Her thoughts drifted to her family. She knew her mother would be happy to see her, yet her mother's habit of scrutinizing her daughter from head to toe, starting with her short hair-do and ending with her ungainly size-nine feet, was a bit unnerving.

But she felt so good after hearing the glowing report from Nurse Marstad, she was determined not to let her mother bother her this time. "I'll just pretend I don't hear her," Cherry decided. "And if she's upset about my leaving so soon, I'll just explain that I'm transporting important medicine!"

She checked her watch. It was after noon, and she felt ready for a good stretch and some lunch. She stopped at a tidy roadside café and stepped out of her car for some quick calisthenics, to the amusement of the other travelers. Cherry was aware that her actions looked odd, but she ignored their giggles. As a nurse, she knew that sitting for too long was bad for the circulation, and a good stretch was the best medicine for sleepy limbs.

After a nourishing lunch of an egg salad sandwich, jello and milk, she purchased steaming coffee in a paper cup and took it to her car. She hoped it would revive her for the last leg of the trip.

Cherry balanced the paper cup on the seat, and while she waited for the coffee to cool, she opened her purse, took out her compact, and reapplied her lipstick. She reached for a tissue from her glove compartment and clumsily knocked over the cup of coffee, spilling it inside her purse and all over Nurse Marstad's important package!

"Oh, dear!" she cried, grabbing the cup before its entire contents could empty into her purse. She used a tissue to wipe the package, but when she did, she erased the name and address right off the brown paper wrapping!

"Jeepers!" she cried. "How am I going to deliver this now? I can't call Nurse Marstad and admit I dropped hot coffee on her package." She looked at the map the head nurse had given her, and was relieved that her destination was clearly marked. "At least I know the town I'm going to," she sighed.

"Now if I can just find the name and address of the person who's supposed to get this. Maybe their name is on the inside," she thought brightly.

Cherry carefully untied the string holding the parcel together. Inside the brown-paper wrapper was Lana's book! "Why, this isn't medicine!" Cherry cried. "Nurse Marstad must have goofed and given me the wrong package!" Although it was hard for Cherry to believe that Nurse Marstad *ever* made a mistake!

While she was loath to call her boss and admit she had opened the parcel, she knew, as a nurse, she was bound to deliver that special experimental medication!

"Even if I have to turn around and drive all the way back to Seattle General Hospital, I'll do it," she declared. "For there's no such thing as a vacation from helping others!" She hopped out of her car and made a bee-line to the nearest public telephone. She fished through her wet purse for the correct change, and a minute later, she was on the line to the main desk at Seattle General Hospital.

"I'd like to speak to Head Nurse Margaret Marstad, please," she said in a shaky voice.

"I'm sorry, miss," the operator replied. "Nurse Marstad is on vacation."

"How queer!" Cherry frowned. Why, she knew Nurse Marstad had just come back from a vacation.

"I'll transfer you to our replacement head nurse. Hold, please."

In a minute, Nurse Gerry George was on the phone. "I need to speak to Nurse Marstad," Cherry said, trying not to sound frantic. "It's very important."

"I'm sorry, Cherry, but Nurse Marstad is gone."

"Did she leave a message for me?" Cherry asked, not wishing to give away the nature of her call. "About a package?"

"She didn't leave a message for anyone. It was the queerest thing. I got to work at eleven and was told I would be the replacement head nurse for a while. I've got to go, Cherry. Golly, I never realized how hard Marstad's job was. Have a great vacation!"

Cherry went back to her car feeling more confused than ever. "What am I going to do?" she wondered. She glared at the book in her hand. "All this trouble," she cried, "over a silly little book!" She tossed it on the seat next to her. A piece of paper fluttered to the floor. "Hmmn. Look, there's a note!" Cherry felt a sense of guilt creeping over her. She was aware she was reading correspondence not meant for her eyes.

Midge—Mother having problems with Father. Holiday plans canceled. Trouble at home. Can you advise?
Pegs

"If Nurse Marstad simply gave me the wrong package, this note wouldn't be in here," she reasoned, remembering that the package had been addressed to a Miss Midge Somebody. "I bet Nurse Marstad went away because of her family troubles, only she was too ashamed to tell anyone about it."

Cherry's heart went out to the gruff-seeming nurse. "She hides a broken heart under all her brusqueness," she thought, tears filling her eyes.

Cherry examined the cover of the book. *The Lost Secrets of the Sisters of Mercy.* Cherry was not a big reader, and religious stories did not appeal to her in the least. Still, the nun on the cover was awfully attractive, she thought.

She opened the book to the inscription page.

"With love from G.A. to C.M.," it said.

"This proves this is Lana's book, for these are the same initials I saw engraved on her ring!" Cherry exclaimed. "Why did Nurse Marstad claim this book belonged to her?"

Cherry laughed at herself. "I'm sure there's a very simple explanation for all this. Why, I'm starting to think everything's a mystery! I'll just deliver this parcel as promised, and when I get back to the hospital, I'm sure Nurse Marstad will clear all this up."

But she still had a kernel of doubt in the back of her mind.

She decided to have a closer look at the book. "As long as I've already opened it, I might as well have a peek," she reasoned.

She skimmed the first chapter. "I can't quite put my finger on it, but there is something very different about this book!" Cherry mused as she flipped through the pages. Why, except for some men hired to haul heavy furniture in chapter three, all the characters in the book were women! Fascinated, Cherry read on. Before she knew it, more than an hour had passed, and she was a quarter of the way through the book. She was so deeply engrossed she had lost track of the time.

"Oh, dear!" she cried when she finally checked her watch. Cherry prided herself on her promptness, and although she hadn't called her mother to tell her she was coming, she had a schedule of her own to keep!

She put the book on the passenger seat, turned on her engine and put her car in reverse. But she found her exit was blocked by two men in a red convertible. She politely beeped her horn to let the men know they were blocking her way, but instead of moving, the driver got out of the car.

He threw his cigar butt on the ground, buttoned his black overcoat up to his chin and pulled his hat low over his face. He sauntered menacingly over to Cherry's car. His companion had slipped behind the wheel of the convertible and was gunning the engine.

Cherry didn't want to acknowledge the man, but she didn't want to be rude, either. "Perhaps he wants my parking spot," she thought.

"I'm leaving right now," she said in a cheerful tone that belied her true feelings. Frankly, this man gave her the creeps! "There's something about him that seems awfully familiar," Cherry shuddered.

He leaned on Cherry's car in an insolent manner and grinned. He squinted at her through thick black-framed glasses. "What's the hurry, sister? My buddy and I just pulled in here for a nice cold beer. Care to join us?"

"No thanks," Cherry gulped. "I simply must be on my way." The man's fresh attitude angered her, but she tried never to engage in a quarrel.

"Always turn the other cheek," her mother counseled, and those were words Cherry lived by.

The man acted like he hadn't heard her and opened her car door. Cherry gasped indignantly. "How rude," she cried. "If you don't quit pestering me, I'll be forced to call for assistance!" she declared.

Beep! Beep! A large man wearing a loud Hawaiian shirt and driving a wood-paneled station wagon full of noisy children was trying to squeeze past the two cars. "Hey, buddy, you're blocking the road!" he yelled. "Move it!"

The rude man in the black overcoat scowled, slammed

Cherry's door, and skulked back to his car. Cherry waited a few minutes after they drove off, hoping to put some distance between herself and the rude men. She pulled out of the parking lot and cautiously maneuvered her car through the heavy late-afternoon traffic. It would be dark soon, and although her mother wasn't expecting her, if she happened to call the hospital and find out Cherry had left many hours ago for Idaho, she would surely worry.

She stopped at a service station and drank a refreshing orange soda while a capable young girl with a darling short haircut checked her oil, brake fluid and tires and cleaned her windows.

"Great story," the girl said, pointing to the book on the seat next to Cherry. "You'll love the ending."

"I can't wait to finish it," Cherry enthused, waving good-bye to the friendly girl. She put all thoughts of the two rude men out of her head and concentrated on the miles ahead of her.

So many peculiar things had happened to her in the last few days. "Once I get to San Francisco I can really relax!" she thought happily.

CHAPTER 4

What a Conundrum

When Cherry pulled into the driveway of the tidy split-level house at 17 Badger Avenue, it was just after eight p.m. She knew her mother would be finishing the dinner dishes while her father sat in his easy chair, *The Pleasantville Times* in one hand and a highball in the other.

She wanted to surprise them, but Lady heard the car pull into the driveway, and her barking drew Mrs. Aimless to the screen door.

"It's Cherry! Cherry's come home!" her mother exclaimed as she flew out the front door with Lady at her heels. They raced across the front yard, Mrs. Aimless staying on the tidy brick path but Lady bounding exuberantly through the flower bed. Lady reached Cherry first, and in her enthusiasm muddied Cherry's skirt.

"Oh, I wish I had known you were coming! Why, the house is such a mess! Oh, dear!" cried Mrs. Aimless, holding her daughter at arms length while looking her up and down. She brushed the mud from Cherry's outfit. "Oh, I wish I could keep this dog out of my petunias. She's ruined your skirt. Well, never mind; I never did like that shade of blue on you anyway!" The collie jumped around the two, barking with pleasure.

"And I must look a sight!" she added, taking off her apron to reveal an immaculately-tailored cream-colored shirt-waist with a scoop collar that set off her tan to perfection.

Cherry grinned. Same old mom! She hugged the older woman and assured her that she looked just fine. But Cherry was fibbing, for despite the deep tan and attractive coiffure, Mrs. Aimless looked tired. Cherry hoped her absence wasn't putting those worry lines across her mother's forehead.

"Is Father home?" Cherry asked, retrieving her luggage and purse from the car.

Her mother frowned. "He's had a bad day at work, and he's in one of his moods," she warned. "I'd wait until he speaks to you before bothering him. Let's go in the back way so we don't disturb him."

Cherry followed her mother to the back door. Once in the kitchen, they relaxed over some key lime pie and coffee. Cherry began chatting happily about her work in Seattle but was interrupted several times by questions from her mother.

"Do you have to wear those ugly white nurse's shoes, dear?"

"Do all nurses have such short hair?"

"Have you met any attractive doctors?"

Each time Cherry tried to open her mouth, her mother interrupted with another question. Could it be that her mother didn't want to hear about her nurse chums and their fascinating patients?

Cherry suddenly felt very tired. It had been a long drive, and her pleasure at being home had dissolved during her mother's interrogation. A good night's sleep will cheer me up, she thought, barely stifling a yawn.

Her mother shooed her off to bed. "There's plenty of time for catching up, dear," she said, kissing her good-night. "Why, we've got almost two whole weeks together!"

Cherry didn't have the heart to tell her mother she was going to be in Pleasantville for only a day. She was glad she had agreed to deliver Nurse Marstad's package. She didn't feel quite as selfish, knowing she was going to do something important for someone else. Somehow she'd make her mother understand.

CHAPTER 5

An Odd Occurrence

Cherry snuggled under the quilt Aunt Gertrude had made for her and yawned. Finally, it felt right to be home, safe and snug in her little attic bedroom with Lady sprawled at her feet. She was just drifting off to sleep when Lady jumped off the bed and raced to the door. "She seems awfully agitated about something," Cherry thought as she slipped out of her warm bed, donned her pink chenille robe and fuzzy slippers, and quietly crept downstairs with Lady at her heels.

Once downstairs, the collie gave a little yelp and ran to the den, where Mr. Aimless lay fast asleep in his recliner, the pages of the evening paper scattered at his feet.

"It's freezing in here," Cherry shuddered, covering her father with a comforter from the davenport.

"Why, the window's open!" she exclaimed, creeping across the room to close it, taking care not to wake her father. "Mother always closes this before she goes to bed; the wind must have blown it open. Good thing the noise woke Lady; otherwise Father might have caught a terrible cold—or worse!" She latched the window firmly.

But the collie still seemed agitated. She climbed on Mrs. Aimless's favorite chair—an act which was strictly forbidden in the spotless Aimless house—peered out the window and growled. Cherry looked, too, but saw nothing but a quiet little street lined with majestic maple trees.

"That's funny," she thought. "It's not windy at all."

"There's no one out there, girl," Cherry said, scratching Lady behind the ears. "Hush." She certainly didn't want her father awakening in a grumpy mood, especially since tomorrow she would tell him she was going to visit her Aunt Gertrude.

"Let's go back to bed," she said, tugging gently on her pet's collar. Cherry stopped in the living room long enough to find something to read, in case she couldn't get back to sleep. All she could find stacked in tidy piles on the kidney-shaped coffee table were fashion magazines and several issues of *Reader's Digest*. Nothing piqued her interest.

"I haven't finished Lana's book yet!" she suddenly remembered, going to the kitchen to get her purse. But it wasn't on the table where she had left it earlier. "Mother must have moved it," Cherry reasoned, noticing how tidy the kitchen was. But her purse wasn't in the front hall closet, nor was it in the deacon's bench in the entryway, where her mother stored her spare handbags. She found it in the tiny room off the garage that served as her mother's laundry room. The contents of the purse, including the book, had been placed in a neat row on the ironing board.

"Mother is such a dear," Cherry smiled. "She must have discovered that I spilled coffee in my handbag and cleaned it after I went to bed." She took the book and crept back upstairs, pulling a reluctant Lady behind her. Cherry settled in for a good read, but before she could finish even one page, she was fast asleep. But for Lady, there was no such slumber. She maintained her guard all through the night from her station at the foot of Cherry's bed.

She knew there was something out there in the night, even if her mistress didn't!

Cherry awoke to brilliant sunlight streaming across her face. Lady was awake and waiting patiently on the rag rug beside the bed. "Rise and shine!" her mother called from the kitchen. From the fragrant smells wafting up the stairs, Cherry could tell her mother was preparing her award-winning strawberry waffles. She jumped out of bed, donned a simple kelly green dress with a sweetheart neckline, and raced down the stairs, taking them two at a time. Why, she hadn't had a decent waffle for a whole year!

Cherry spent the morning in a whirlwind: chatting on the phone with chums, standing still so her mother could measure her for a new party frock, and making rhubarb tarts for her mother's bridge club luncheon the next day. Mid-afternoon she slipped into a gingham sundress and soft white moccasins and walked downtown. The heat was stifling, and she ducked into Tilly's Drugstore for a refreshing vanilla soda. She was just deciding whether or not to have a second, when Miss

Molly Mathers, the high school physical education teacher, plopped down onto the stool beside her. She was so full of questions about life in a big city hospital that before Cherry knew it, two hours had slipped away.

"Golly," she gulped, taking a last sip of her second soda. "I've got to get home to help Mother prepare supper. Bye, Miss Mathers."

Cherry ran all the way back to Badger Avenue and found her mother had everything under control. The dining room table had already been set with the good china, and azaleas from Mrs. Aimless's garden had been arranged in a festive centerpiece at the center of the table.

Cherry took a quick shower, ran a comb through her disheveled curls and applied fresh lipstick. Resplendent in a dressy mint-green crepe frock and festive gold sandals, she made her way downstairs. "Why, I forgot to eat lunch!" she exclaimed, sniffing appreciatively. Her mother had prepared a special supper of pot roast, baked potatoes and green bean casserole. A strawberry cake sat cooling in the kitchen, awaiting a final frosting of vanilla icing.

Mrs. Aimless sent her daughter into the living room to finish arranging the hors d'oeuvres. Mr. and Mrs. Cleaver, her parent's closest friends, arrived a few minutes later.

"Why, Cherry, you look splendid!" gushed Mrs. Cleaver, hugging the blushing girl to her cashmere-clad bosom. "And, Doris, your table could win a prize!" Mrs. Cleaver complimented Mrs. Aimless, who beamed with pride.

Mr. Aimless was delayed at the office, so Cherry, her mother and their guests sat patiently in the living room, sampling the yummy treats her mother had spent the afternoon preparing.

"Delicious cheese ball!" Mr. Cleaver exclaimed. Mrs. Aimless confessed that she was testing a new recipe for entry in the upcoming county fair. Her guests assured her she would surely win first prize, and reached for seconds. Half a cheese ball later, Mr. Aimless arrived and dinner was served.

Mrs. Aimless seated Cherry next to her father. "Have a nice chat with your father," she whispered in Cherry's ear.

Cherry made several attempts to engage her father in conversation and finally got him talking with a query about his business. A long lecture about the booming real estate market in Idaho followed. Cherry found her mind wandering to the absent Aimless—her twin brother Charles.

How she wished Charley were here! Although the two didn't look anything alike, Charley being as fair as she was dark, they shared the same sense of fun and good sportsmanship. Charley was so animated and funny that he had saved many family dinners from complete disaster with his quick wit.

"So, Cherry, how's life in the big city?" asked Mrs. Cleaver, digging into the green bean and potato chip casserole. "Your mother tells me you work with lots of interesting doctors!"

"*Single* doctors," her mother added, winking at her friend. Cherry wanted to talk about her hospital experiences, about her friends and the mysterious Lana, but she knew any mention of a mystery would just worry her mother, who had never forgotten the fright she had experienced during the Pringle farm incident.

That adventure had scared Cherry, too, for she had been kidnapped and tied up in a fruit cellar. She still shuddered when she remembered the feeling of spiders crawling over her arms and legs! It was only because of the heroic Lady that the search party had found Cherry. The collie had tunneled her way out of the cellar and run miles through pouring rain for help.

Cherry slipped the courageous collie a nice piece of pot roast. The dog accepted the offering gratefully from her hiding place at Cherry's feet. Cherry wiped her hands on the embroidered napkin in her lap. As she fingered the linen she fondly remembered the summer twelve years ago when her father's sister had come to visit. That summer her Aunt Gertrude taught her to sew, and they had made many lovely things together.

For some reason, Father didn't like his youngest sister and refused to speak of her. But when Mr. Aimless had gone east for the summer to a special real estate school, her mother had invited Aunt Gertrude for a visit.

Gert had never married, but with her vivacious personality and striking good looks, she made friends easily. The first week in Pleasantville she became fast friends with the town librarian, Miss Hathaway. Soon the four of them had become a sort of club, and they spent the summer days swimming, hiking, and picnicking. In the evening, they had often sat on the front porch, sewing and talking.

Her father had arrived home a week early to find Gert and Miss Hathaway napping in the spare bedroom. He forbade them to set foot in his house again, and that was the last Cherry saw of Aunt Gert. Her parents didn't know they had been writing regularly since Cherry went away to nursing school.

Her mother interrupted her thoughts. Apparently, she had been trying to get Cherry's attention for some time. "So, Cherry, what are you planning to do with the rest of your vacation? There's plenty going on here, what with the county fair coming up, and the hay ride, and that nice young Jim Fud has been asking about you."

"Why, I'm going to visit Aunt Gertrude in San Francisco!" Cherry blurted out before she could stop herself.

Cherry held her breath. The room seemed so still. No one said a word. Finally, her mother broke the silence.

"San Francisco? Isn't that awfully far away?" her mother asked nervously.

She was interrupted by shouts from a group of Cherry's chums, five good-natured, if somewhat noisy, girls who had just pulled up in a canary-yellow sedan. The group had spent all their spare time together in high school, leaving no room for the school activities, football games and Saturday night dates that other girls were so interested in.

Many a time Mrs. Aimless had counseled Cherry that no man would want to marry her if she didn't begin to act more interested in dating, but Cherry had brushed her off with a joking, "So who wants to get married?"

"I suppose marriage isn't for everyone," Mrs. Aimless had told herself. "After all, Gertrude seems happy enough." Cherry was relieved that her chums had provided her with a polite exit. "Sorry, Mom, but I told the gang to come by after supper. I won't be out late." With this, the pretty young nurse threw a white beaded sweater over her shoulders and flew out the door to join her friends.

Over a chocolate sundae, Cherry filled her friends in on the mysterious events of the last few days. "Although I don't know exactly what's going on, I still have to deliver this package to Oregon. Why, that's halfway to San Francisco. I couldn't change my mind now if I wanted to. Which I don't," she added somewhat ruefully. "All I know is, my parents don't like the idea."

"Oh, go, Cherry, go," said Dessa, a darling brown-eyed girl with a snub nose and a smattering of freckles across her face. "You've got two weeks' pay and a place to stay—why, that head nurse practically ordered you to go!"

"And you know how you love to obey orders, Nurse Aimless," giggled Beth, the athlete of the group, whose strong shoulders attested to her love of swimming. "Cherry, you need a break, and staying here with your family is no vacation," she continued in a more serious tone.

"They're right," broke in Arlene, a raven-haired beauty with a beguiling smile and a forthright manner. "Pleasantville is not exactly the most exciting place on the planet!"

Cherry licked the last bit of chocolate sauce from her spoon, and ordered another sundae. If she was going to stand up to her parents, she'd better get more courage—and quick!

When she arrived home, her mother was sitting at the kitchen table, absent-mindedly looking through a recipe book. Her father was asleep on the davenport, the evening paper spread at his feet. Cherry steeled herself for her mother's reaction to her trip, but before she could open her mouth, her mother surprised her.

"If you're going, you'd better get to bed soon, dear," Mrs. Aimless said, shutting *The Joy of Cooking* and placing it back on the shelf.

Cherry jumped up and down with glee. "You mean you don't mind? And Father too?"

"I made a deal with your father. He lets you visit Gert, and

I promise not to put arsenic in his coffee!" The twinkle in her eye let Cherry in on the joke, and they had a good laugh.

"Oh," squealed Cherry. "There's so much to do! I've got dirty clothes to wash, and I promised Aunt Gert I'd call her tonight."

Her mother interrupted. "While you were out with your friends I did your laundry; it's all ironed and pressed and on your bed. And I called Gert, but she wasn't home."

"That's funny," Cherry said. "Tonight was the night we set aside to talk. She wanted to know exactly when I was arriving so she could be home."

"You know your Aunt Gert sometimes forgets where she's supposed to be. She always has her head in the clouds, just like someone else I know." Mrs. Aimless grinned and shook her head. "You always were like two peas in a pod," she said. "The older you get, the more you become like Gert. Why, I was just telling her last week that when I look at you, sometimes I swear I see her."

Cherry was amazed. "You and Aunt Gert keep in touch?"

Mrs. Aimless smiled. "What your father doesn't know..."

"...won't hurt him!" Cherry grinned, sweeping her mother up in her arms for a quick waltz around the kitchen table. She deposited a dizzy Mrs. Aimless on the yellow Formica countertop.

Cherry hugged her mother, who was turning out to be more of an ally than she had imagined. She tried to put her thanks into words. "I know it's hard for you, with Charley and me so far away..."

Her mother hugged her back, and wiped a little tear from her eye. "I guess we've all got to follow our rainbows, dear. Now, off to bed with you!" she said, playfully pushing Cherry toward the stairs. "Oh, and Cherry, I put that lavender handkerchief back in the pocket of your uniform. Who on earth is M.M.?"

But Cherry wasn't listening. She was too excited to hear anything but the plans buzzing in her head. She didn't know how she was ever going to sleep! "I'm really, truly going to San Francisco," she whispered as she raced up the stairs to her attic room. She didn't know why, but she had a feeling something very special was awaiting her in the city by the bay!

CHAPTER 6

A Quick Escape

Cherry had set her alarm for six a.m. in order to get an early start on her trip, but when she awoke, she found she was more tired than she had anticipated. "Just ten more minutes' sleep," she groaned, pulling the covers firmly over her head and settling into the soft feather mattress. When she awoke again, her little attic room was flooded with sunlight. The clock read seven-fifteen.

"Goodness!" she cried, bolting out of bed. "I'd better hurry." Cherry quickly bathed and ran a comb through her tousled curls. From her suitcase she selected a bright yellow poplin dress with a flared skirt that she knew would be comfortable to sit in as well as pleasing to the eye. She slipped Lana's book into one of the wide front pockets, grabbed her luggage and ran downstairs, as always taking the steps two at a time.

"Good morning, early bird," her mother teased her sleepy-eyed daughter. Mrs. Aimless had tied a white apron over a flowered housecoat and was cutting thick slices of homemade white bread. Cherry's purse was sitting on the kitchen table, its interior clean and dry.

"I'm sending a hamper of food with you," Mrs. Aimless said, making cream cheese and jelly sandwiches to add to the bag of fruit and generous slices of strawberry cake already in the wicker hamper. Cherry assured her that there would be food along the way, but her mother just shook her head.

"You never know what's in restaurant food these days," she said, "especially in those roadside places. One or two eggs?" she asked, holding up a bowl of hard-boiled eggs.

"Two," Cherry said, pouring herself a cup of coffee.

"Be careful about drinking the water in California. I hear it's full of chemicals. And drive carefully. If you get sleepy, pull off the road. Don't speak to strangers. I've put a couple of clean towels over there on the chair. It's best if you use towels from home."

"Yes, Mother," Cherry said, quickly draining her cup of coffee and snatching a piece of dry toast. Before her mother could talk her into sitting down for a big breakfast, Cherry picked up the hamper of food and her luggage, hugged her mother, and sailed out the door.

"Call me as soon as you get there!" her mother cried after her.

"I will," Cherry said, her mouth full of toast.

"Don't forget what I told you!" Mrs. Aimless cried.

"I won't."

"And have a good time," she waved. But her good wishes came too late, for her daughter was already backing out of the driveway. Sometimes Mrs. Aimless thought her daughter was entirely too independent for her own good, gallivanting around the Northwest the way she did. It pleased her to know that Cherry's twin, Charley, was settled in a good job in the interior design business in New York, even if it was so far away. She did wonder, however, if he was ever going to settle down and get married, or if he was planning on living with that roommate for the rest of his life.

Why, he and Johnny had even bought a house together! She had warned them that someday one of them would marry, and then where would the other one be? But Charley had just laughed and told her not to worry. And she didn't worry as much about Charley as she did about Cherry. After all, twenty-four wasn't old for a boy to be unmarried, considering that they matured later than girls.

Mrs. Aimless poured herself another cup of coffee and opened the morning paper. "Same news as yesterday," she sighed, scanning the front page of the *Idaho Daily Gazette*.

"Oh, dear!" she cried, "What's this?"

"'The nuns of the Sisters of Mercy convent, located eighty miles north of San Francisco, have been missing for two days and are now feared to be the victims of a mass kidnapping,'" Mrs. Aimless read aloud. A photo of the Mother Superior accompanied the article. "Why, she's very attractive, for a nun," Mrs. Aimless mused. "She could be a movie star!"

"Good thing Cherry didn't see this story," Mrs. Aimless thought. "If she knew there was a mystery brewing near San

Francisco, she'd drive twice as fast so she could get in on it," she chuckled. She put the paper aside. "I'll worry about Cherry later," she told herself, getting out her mixing bowls and cake tins. "Right now I've got work to do."

As her mother was stirring angel food cake batter, Cherry was turning onto the main road that would take her out of Pleasantville and towards Oregon. If all went well, she would be in San Francisco late the following night.

"I still haven't called Aunt Gertrude!" she yelped, making a mental note to do so at her first rest stop. She remembered the last time she had seen her aunt, an attractive, lively woman with short wavy black hair and those famous Aimless eyes— big and green and sparkling with life. Gert, the youngest of seven, was only seventeen years older than her look-alike niece.

"We're so much alike, you could be my own daughter," her aunt had murmured when they said good-bye twelve years ago. Cherry hadn't replied, but in her heart she was pleased at being compared with such an intelligent, lively person. "I'd give anything to be even a little like Aunt Gert," Cherry thought with a smile. She flicked on the radio for company and concentrated on the road ahead.

After an uneventful day, Cherry found herself on the out-skirts of Warm Springs, where she was to deliver Nurse Marstad's package. During the drive, she had devised a plan to find the recipient of the parcel.

"When I get to the town, I'll go through the telephone directory. If I'm lucky, this Midge person will have her full name and address listed." She pulled off the highway and headed towards the center of town. She was anxious to test her idea and a little afraid that it wouldn't work. "After all, not every person has a telephone," she reminded herself. She crossed her fingers. With Nurse Marstad on vacation, this was the only possible way she could find this Midge person. "It's just got to work!" she exclaimed.

She soon reached the center of town, which was alive with afternoon shoppers strolling under old oak trees. "What a darling little town!" Cherry exclaimed, parking her Buick in a shady spot in front of Mr. Stanley's Sweet Shoppe. She hopped out of her car, smoothed the wrinkles in her dress, and peered in the window. She didn't see a telephone, but she could smell the most delicious aromas coming from inside.

"Perhaps a nutritious snack will calm my nerves," she thought, realizing that many hours had passed since her skimpy breakfast of coffee and dry toast. Once inside the sweet-smelling shop, painted cotton-candy pink, Cherry was greeted by Mr. Stanley himself, dressed in a neat pink and white striped smock.

Cherry took her time selecting an assortment of chocolates. "Coconut cremes or caramels?" she wondered, furrowing her pretty brow. She laughed when she caught a glimpse of herself in the mirror behind the counter. "I look so serious," she thought. "Just a few days ago, I was making life-or-death decisions, and today I'm selecting candy with the same earnestness!

"Although, when a girl's ready to get her visitor, sometimes chocolate can be pretty serious," Cherry had to admit.

She finally selected a well-rounded assortment of chocolates and paid for them with the money from Nurse Marstad. She leaned on the cool white marble counter, and while she waited for her change, surveyed the neat little store, decorated in many shades of pink. A roll of pink striped paper next to the register gave her an idea. Cherry fished Lana's book from her pocket. "What would be the fee to wrap this?" she asked.

"No charge. Gift wrap is free with any purchase," Mr. Stanley replied in a genial manner. He swiftly wrapped the book, topping off the package with a thin gold ribbon. He used a small scissors that he kept on a chain around his neck to transform the flat ribbon into a cascade of curls.

"It's lovely!" Cherry exclaimed. Nurse Marstad's package

no longer resembled the plain, brown-paper parcel Cherry had begun her journey with, but at least she wouldn't have to hand over an unwrapped book.

"Now all I have to do is find a quiet telephone booth where I can begin my search for Midge," she thought. As she left the shop, she heard a cry for help. An elderly woman lay injured on the sidewalk!

Cherry raced to her side and found that the woman was alert but badly frightened. After determining that she had no broken bones, Cherry gingerly helped her to her feet. "What happened?" Cherry cried. "I'm a nurse!"

"A rude man knocked me down!" the woman declared. Cherry looked around, but saw no one. She led the woman, who was attired in a smart gray worsted wool suit with pearl accessories, into the sweet shop and seated her in a comfortable chair. While Cherry talked to the woman in soothing tones, she efficiently took her pulse, using her sturdy nurse's watch. "She's upset, but not dangerously so," Cherry decided.

Mr. Stanley brought a tray of tea and ladyfingers. "Now what happened, dear?" he asked.

The elderly woman took a lace handkerchief from her modern black handbag and wiped her brow. "I had just had my hair set by Mr. Francis across the street, and I was headed here to get some vanilla wafers, when I had the unfortunate luck to collide with a terrible man wearing a long black coat! Mr. Stanley, I think he was headed toward your shop. When I called for help, he ran the other way. Goodness, he was in a hurry!

"I'm not hurt, but I fear he's ruined my hair!"

"Your hair looks fabulous," Mr. Stanley enthused. Cherry took her compact from her purse and showed the woman that her upswept hair-do was indeed in perfect order.

The woman shook her head. "The police ought to round up all the rude men and put them behind bars!" she declared. Mr. Stanley nodded in agreement. "Why, I had an encounter with a rude man just the other day," Cherry remembered.

The woman sipped her tea, and in a few minutes, her cheeks were rosy again. "I'm Miss Masie Miller, and thanks to you two, I'm feeling much better. I'd like both of you to be my guests at dinner tonight."

Much as Cherry wanted to join the fun, she had a mission

to complete. Mr. Stanley admitted that he didn't keep an up-to-date telephone directory in his shop but directed Cherry to a nearby establishment that was sure to have what she needed.

After bidding her new friends good-bye, she walked briskly two blocks east. She found the Miraloma Club and was surprised to find that Mr. Stanley had directed her to a tavern—and a dimly-lit one at that!

Cherry stood at the curb and ate a coconut creme candy. She realized it would be dusk soon. "If I'm going to find this Midge person, I should start soon, while it's still daylight." Still, she hesitated. She hadn't the courage to enter the dark place all by herself.

She frowned. "Cherry, you're being a big baby," she scolded herself. "Nancy Clue wouldn't be afraid to go anywhere if she were hot on the trail of a clue!"

She took a deep breath, squared her shoulders and went inside.

CHAPTER 7

An Amazing Coincidence

 Cherry paused in the narrow entryway of the bar while her eyes adjusted to the dim light. She was looking around the room for a friendly face when a handsome girl playing billiards smiled at her.

Cherry smiled back and walked over to the girl. "I'm looking for a telephone," she said.

The girl took a cigarette from the pack rolled in the sleeve of her white T-shirt. She lit it, leaned against the wall and took a good long look at Cherry. "Why not stay awhile and have a drink?" she suggested, patting the seat of the bar stool next to her.

"Thank you, but I'm not thirsty," Cherry said. "What I need is a telephone."

"I've got a telephone back at my place," the girl replied, between puffs on her cigarette. "You're welcome to it."

"What a nice girl," Cherry thought, realizing that it might take several phone calls before she located Nurse Marstad's friend. A private telephone would certainly be more convenient.

"That would be great!" Cherry cried. "I don't mean to be pushy, but can we go right now?"

The girl whistled low under her breath. "I like pushy," she said, throwing her cue on the pool table and slipping on her leather jacket.

"Brenda is going to kill you!" one of her chums warned her.

"Brenda is visiting her mother in Ohio, remember?" the girl retorted. "So how's she going to know?"

Her friend laughed. "Mickey, you're a fool if you think you can do anything without Brenda knowing about it. Last time you thought you got away with something, you weren't allowed out for a month, remember?"

Mickey scowled and took off her jacket. She looked at Cherry and sighed. "Maybe another time," she said sadly.

Cherry wasn't sure what had just happened, but she had a feeling she was no longer welcome to use the girl's telephone. She returned to the entryway to puzzle over her next move when someone came charging through the door and knocked her right off her feet!

The girl made a gallant attempt to stop Cherry's fall, but she only succeeded in grabbing onto her dress. Cherry blushed when she heard the unmistakable sound of tearing fabric. "Mother's right. Always wear a slip," she thought glumly as she lay on the floor.

"I'm so sorry!" the girl cried, holding out a hand to help the hapless Cherry. "And I've torn your pretty dress!"

When their eyes met, both girls gasped.

"Why, it's like looking into a mirror!" Cherry cried. With her curvaceous figure, dark curly hair and bright green eyes, this girl could be her twin!

"You *do* look just like me!" the girl agreed, helping Cherry up and inspecting her closely.

"Why, we could be sisters!"

Cherry studied the girl's stunning scarlet shift.

"I've never thought of wearing that color!" she exclaimed. "But it looks so good on you!"

"I was just admiring the color of your dress," the girl laughed. "It's buttercup-yellow, isn't it? Gee, I hope I didn't ruin it."

Just then a handsome blond-haired girl, nattily attired in men's slacks and a white cotton button-down shirt, gave Cherry a teasing pinch.

"Hi, baby," she whispered, in a familiar manner. "Did you miss me?"

When Cherry jumped and squeaked "Who are you?" the girl realized her mistake.

"Golly, there's two of you? I can't believe what I'm seeing!" she exclaimed, quickly taking her hand off Cherry's hip. "Velma, you didn't tell me you had a sister!" she cried, looking rather flustered.

Cherry and her look-a-like burst into peals of laughter.

"Neither did my parents," Velma joked. "What a funny thing! I come in to meet you and end up meeting my long-lost twin!"

"It was the queerest thing," Cherry added, explaining the circumstances of their meeting.

Velma suggested they step outside so she could assess the damage to Cherry's dress. On the way out, the tall blonde bumped into the girl with the pool cue, and soon a heated discussion ensued. Velma pulled at her friend's shirt sleeve. "Let's get out of here," she said. But the girl didn't budge. Cherry hoped there wasn't going to be a fight!

Velma put her hands on her hips and stomped her daintily-clad feet. "You promised you wouldn't fight any more!" she cried. "I'm leaving!" She grabbed Cherry's hand and marched out the door. The tall blonde raced after them, trying to explain.

"That pool shark made a filthy remark about you being twins!" she cried. "I was just defending your honor."

Velma pouted prettily when she heard this. Cherry could see all was forgiven.

"Okay, Miss Midge Fontaine, but in the future..."

"Your name is Midge?" Cherry cried. "Oh, I'm sorry to interrupt, but I'm supposed to deliver a package to someone named Midge, only I don't know her last name. Are there a lot of Midges in this town?" she wondered aloud, adding, "My boss, Head Nurse Miss Marstad, asked me to deliver a package on my way to San Francisco."

"I have a friend named Nurse Marstad!" Midge cried. "Why, that package must be for me!"

"This is almost too good to be true!" Cherry said, relieved to be finally delivering the package. She took the gift-wrapped book from her purse and presented it to Midge.

"How odd," Midge said. "My birthday's not for another month." She looked quizzically at the fancy package. "Peg's gone all frou-frou on me," she joked, tearing at the pink-striped paper. When she saw the book, she exclaimed, "How queer! This is the same book she sent me last year! She must be losing her memory."

Cherry waited anxiously for Midge to open the book and find the note, but Midge just slipped it into her jacket pocket.

"Should I tell her about the note?" Cherry wondered. She shifted uncomfortably in her shoes. "That note was private," she thought guiltily. "Maybe I'd better not. Maybe Midge will find it," she hoped. "But what if she doesn't! Golly, that note seemed important!"

Velma broke into her thoughts. "Why don't you come home

with us, and we'll get that rip in your dress sewn up," she suggested brightly. "We live just around the corner, and Midge just bought me a nifty new sewing machine."

"That would be swell!" Cherry cried. She looked glumly at the long tear in her skirt. "I do have a sewing kit in my purse, but this is an awfully big rip to mend by hand." Secretly she was relieved at her luck.

"I'll find a way to get Midge to look at that book," she schemed. "If by the end of the evening she hasn't discovered the note on her own, I'll confess."

"My, it's getting chilly," Velma remarked, taking a white chiffon scarf from her purse and wrapping it around her hairdo. "Let's go," she said, linking arms with both girls and propelling them down the sidewalk.

"At least now I can tell you two apart," Midge grinned. She stopped in her tracks. "But wait! I like to know a girl's name before I bring her home," she cracked.

Velma playfully punched Midge on the shoulder. "Yes, what is your name?" she asked.

"It's Cherry."

Midge laughed, then hastily covered up her laugh with a cough. "Uh...that's an unusual name," she said.

"The summer I was born my mother's cherry pie won first prize at the county fair. I'm just lucky it wasn't rhubarb." Cherry grinned. The girls laughed.

"Speaking of pie, I sure could use a snack," Midge declared.

Cherry had an idea. "I have a hamper full of delicious food waiting in my car," she exclaimed. "Maybe later we can have a picnic. But I'll need help finding my car. I'm all turned around. I'm afraid I may be lost."

At this, Midge chuckled. "You don't have to explain to us

that you're lost. Why, you look like a kitten who's wandered too far from the litter."

Cherry blushed.

Velma laughed and squeezed Cherry's arm. "Oh, don't let Midge bother you; comparing you to an animal is one of her highest compliments."

"I didn't mean any harm," Midge said soothingly. "You just come with us."

"But I can't go on a picnic in this ripped dress!" Cherry cried.

"Don't worry, we'll fix everything," Velma said.

Midge and Velma directed Cherry to a pretty little cottage surrounded by tall fir trees. "This is it," Velma said, taking her key from her clutch purse. She opened the door cautiously. As she did, a black and white cocker spaniel stuck its head through the opening and barked a happy greeting.

"This is Eleanor," Midge said, introducing Cherry to a small dog with beautiful round black eyes. The dog extended her dainty paw in the most charming manner, then jumped up and licked Cherry squarely on the nose.

As the three girls entered the cozy living room, decorated in tasteful Danish modern, they were greeted by more barks and yelps. Five adorable puppies came tumbling down the stairs. "Oh, they're so cute!" Cherry cried, kneeling down to pet the spotted pups.

"Midge found Eleanor in the woods one day and brought her home to give birth on my best cashmere sweater," Velma explained. She frowned at Midge in a make-pretend way, then grinned. "Why, this girl is so animal crazy, I swear she drives around looking for strays to bring home."

"Bring home, bring home," came a high-pitched, sing-song voice from the next room.

Cherry jumped. "Who's that?"

"That's our bird, Pearl," Midge and Velma said in unison.

"A bird! Who else do you have here?"

Midge ticked off the pets on her fingers. "There's Chuck the guinea pig, Faye the rabbit, Eleanor and her five puppies, Pearl, Gray Cat..."

"...the mice who live in the cracker boxes in our cupboard..." broke in Velma.

"...and Mary."

Velma turned to Midge. "Who's Mary?"

"A turtle. She's in the bathtub. She's new. And that's it."

"And now you have me," said Cherry.

The girls laughed, pleased to have a new pal.

"Let's see if I can mend your dress, Cherry," Velma said. She went upstairs and returned with a simple black frock that fit Cherry to perfection. Cherry and Midge got acquainted while Velma went to her sewing room to mend the tear.

Midge served cocoa and cookies, while Cherry babbled happily about Seattle General Hospital. "Why, until recently, I was terrified of Nurse Marstad," she admitted. At this, Midge laughed merrily. Apparently, she and the head nurse were old friends.

"Oh, old Peg just acts bossy so the doctors will be afraid of her. She's really a great big marshmallow, especially when it comes to nurses," Midge declared.

Cherry agreed. "She was so nice the other day when I lost a patient. Why, I thought I was going to be fired, but instead I got to go on vacation, as planned." Cherry sipped the delicious cocoa.

"It must be horrible when a patient dies," Midge said sympathetically. "Of course Peg wouldn't fire you!"

"Oh, no," Cherry explained. "Nobody died. I mean, I really *lost* a patient. She disappeared right from the ward. It was so strange. She was sitting in bed talking to a nun, and when I left the ward for a minute, Lana disappeared."

"Wait, who's Lana?" Midge asked. "I'm confused."

"Lana's the amnesia patient who disappeared, but her name's not really Lana," Cherry said. "We called her that because she looks just like Lana Turner!"

"Oh my god!" Midge cried, almost tipping over her cocoa. She steadied her cup and calmed her voice. "I mean, golly. Lana Turner? Really? How interesting. Did you say something about a nun?"

Cherry repeated her story. "Come to think of it, she was the biggest nun I've ever seen," she added. "And rather unfriendly. The priest was a lot nicer."

"There was a priest, too?" Midge asked, raising one eyebrow. Her voice had a casual tone, but Cherry could see that her story had piqued Midge's interest.

Cherry continued. "When I ran into the hallway to see if someone needed help, no one was there except this priest. And he said he hadn't heard anything. He was very nice," Cherry said, adding, "Although, I have to admit, priests make me a little nervous."

"Yeah, they make me nervous too," Midge muttered. "Tell me, what did he look like?"

"He was dressed all in black," she said.

Midge groaned. "Is that it?" she asked impatiently.

"He was wearing thick black-framed glasses," Cherry added helpfully.

Midge jumped up from the table and started pacing around the tiny kitchen. She yanked the book from her jacket pocket and flipped through it. "Phew!" Cherry breathed a sigh of relief. Midge had found the note!

As Midge read, a flash of anxiety crossed her face. Cherry held her breath. She could tell that there was something very wrong!

Midge dropped the book on the table and grinned at Cherry. It was a forced grin, Cherry thought.

"Tell me more about working at the hospital, Cherry," Midge said casually. So Cherry chatted on about her nurse friends and her many patients, but all the while she had the feeling that Midge wasn't really listening. Her thoughts seemed to be elsewhere.

A minute later, Velma came skipping down the stairs. She was wearing Cherry's mended frock, which looked stunning on her. She danced around the tiny kitchen, admiring the way the full skirt twirled above her soft, curvy legs.

"I hope you don't mind that I put it on," she said. "I just love the color!"

"Be my guest," Cherry said. "After all, you were kind enough to loan me this lovely frock."

Velma noticed a loose thread hanging from the hem. "I'm going back upstairs to put the finishing touches on this mending job. Say, Cherry, why don't you stay the night? That way you can make a fresh start in the morning. I'll just put some fresh linens on Midge's bed and you can have her room."

"But I don't want to put anyone out! I can sleep on the couch," she said, nervously eyeing the uncomfortable-looking white vinyl sectional. "I certainly can't expect anyone to give up their room for me."

"No, no, no, no, no," Midge reassured the nervous nurse. "It's no trouble at all. I don't mind sleeping with Velma. Really."

Cherry saw that Midge meant what she said. She was touched by their hospitality and told them so.

"Hey, what's a fellow Girl Scout for?" Midge shrugged.

"How could you tell?" wondered Cherry aloud.

"Oh, we can always spot another Scout," said Midge, winking at Velma.

"While you girls are finishing the dress, I'm going to walk Eleanor," Midge said, hopping up from the table and putting on her jacket.

"Come on, girl. Time for a walk," she called to the cocker spaniel, who was fast asleep on the sectional sofa.

"I could go with you. We can walk Eleanor to my car and then all drive back together!" Cherry cried. "All my things are in the car, so I have to go out anyway."

Midge looked hesitant. "Um, I...Well, to be honest, I always take a walk when I need to think. I won't be very good company," she admitted.

"I'll be as quiet as a mouse," Cherry promised. "Velma, is it okay that I wear your dress?"

Velma nodded and handed Cherry a jacket and her chiffon scarf. "Better bundle up. It gets awfully chilly here at night."

With that settled, Midge put a leash on Eleanor, and off they went.

It was a quiet walk to Cherry's car. Midge appeared to be deep in thought. Besides a few questions about the mysterious disappearance at the hospital, which Cherry answered in as brief a manner as possible, Midge said nothing. They walked for about twenty minutes, going slowly so the dog could take her time and sniff interesting spots.

"Babies are hard work, aren't they?" Midge murmured as she scratched behind the dog's ears.

"What a nice girl," thought Cherry. "I hope that someday I have a roommate just like her." When they got to Cherry's car, Midge lifted Eleanor into the back seat. The three of them made their way home, not realizing that trouble lay ahead.

CHAPTER 8

Kidnapped!

"What's this?" Cherry exclaimed as she reached the darkened front stoop and found the door ajar.

"There's been a break-in!" she cried, her keen eyes noticing the forced lock. "And the porch bulb has been unscrewed."

Midge dashed into the house and called for Velma, but there was no reply.

There was a crash from upstairs. Midge flew up the staircase with Cherry at her heels. Next to Velma's bed was a little gray cat, lapping up spilt milk.

"Oh, kitty!" Midge cried, scooping up the shards of glass before the cat could cut her paws. Cherry searched the rest of the house, but Velma was nowhere to be found! She ran back upstairs to join Midge, who was standing in the middle of Velma's room staring at the bed. "Midge, could it be Velma's gone out for a walk?" Cherry asked hopefully.

Midge shook her head. "Something suspicious has happened," she said. Tears ran down her face.

"I'll call the police," Cherry said, handing Midge the clean handkerchief she always kept in her purse in case of emergencies.

"No police!" Midge cried.

By the tone in her voice Cherry could tell the desperate girl meant business. What was it about the police that alarmed Midge so?

Suddenly, there was a knock at the door. "Hello? Anyone home?" called a masculine voice.

"Up here!" Midge yelled. "That's our chum Tom," she explained.

The man coming up the stairs was tall and slender with large basset-hound eyes. In his arms was Eleanor.

"Midge, what's going on? The door was wide open and Eleanor was left on the stoop. Is Velma back yet? She left so quickly I didn't even get a chance to say hi."

"You saw Velma!" Midge cried. "Where? When?"

"Velma's mysteriously disappeared," Cherry added solemnly.

"Velma's disappeared? How frightful!" Tom cried.

"Where did you see Velma? What did she say?" Midge asked impatiently.

Tom deposited Eleanor on the bed and sat down. "She was leaving the house when I walked up. I came over to see if you girls wanted to hear my new Sinatra record, but before I could speak to Velma, she got into a car with two men and drove off. I'm sure she saw me, but she didn't wave or anything," he said. "Frankly, my feelings were a little hurt."

"What men? What car?" Midge cried.

Tom shook his head. "No one I've seen before, and believe me, I would have remembered these characters." He shuddered. "One man had on a long black coat that was buttoned all the way up to his chin and a hat pulled low over his face. He looked like a spy or a government worker. I guess some people find that style attractive, but I must say I prefer a softer look." He smoothed the leg of his beige pleated pants, which were pressed with a razor-sharp crease.

Something about Tom's description of the man rang a bell in Cherry. Where had she run into a man clad in a long black overcoat?

"Oh, no!" Cherry shrank back in her chair. "I just remembered! I saw him on the way to Idaho!"

"What?" Midge and Tom chorused.

"Was he driving a shiny red convertible?" asked Cherry excitedly.

"Yes!" Tom admitted.

"What is it, Cherry? What do you know?" Midge asked.

"I had a most unpleasant exchange with an unsavory fellow driving a red convertible back in Washington, not long after leaving the hospital. Oh, dear," Cherry wailed. "I think I'm being followed. Whoever took Velma thought she was me. It's all my fault," she sobbed, collapsing on the bed in tears. "People are always disappearing around me. Why, when I was a dude ranch nurse-in-training, an entire family disappeared and was never found!"

"But why would someone want to kidnap you?" Midge wondered aloud.

"I don't know!" Cherry cried. "I'm just a simple nurse. But, now that I think of it, ever since Lana was kidnapped, strange things have been happening. Maybe I'm just a jinx. First Lana disappears, and now Velma's gone."

"Something strange is going on here, Cherry, but I don't think it's your fault," Midge said. She didn't explain what she meant. She simply sat on the edge of the bed and frowned.

Cherry was puzzled. Midge was being awfully mysterious. But before she could quiz her, Midge jumped up from the bed.

"Something is different about this room. I noticed it the minute I came in, but I haven't figured out what it is yet," she said, peering intently around the bedroom.

Cherry surveyed the charming room, but everything seemed in place. "That's a nice photograph of you on Velma's night stand," she remarked.

"That's it!" Midge cried, giving Cherry a little squeeze. "Cherry, you're a genius!"

"But what..."

Before Cherry could finish her sentence, Midge raced down the stairs. "It's here!" she yelled as she bounded back up the stairs and ran into the bedroom. In her hand was the book from Nurse Marstad.

"What could Lana's book possibly have to do with this?" Cherry blurted out.

"*Lana's* book?" Midge cried. "What do you mean? This is the book *Peg* sent me."

Cherry quickly explained how the book had ended up in Nurse Marstad's hands. "I was so confused when she said it belonged to her, and then, when it showed up as a present for you, I didn't know what to think!"

"That explains a lot of things," Midge said mysteriously.

"I'm awfully confused," Cherry said. "I don't understand."

"On the night stand I had another copy of this very same book—the one Peg gave me last year for my birthday," Midge explained. "I was reading it to Velma last night in bed, er, well, never mind. What's important is that *now* the book is gone! Don't you see?"

Cherry and Tom shook their heads. "Frankly, I'm confused," Tom said. "But then again, a lot of things you girls do confuse me."

"Do I have to draw you two a picture?" Midge sighed impatiently. Tom and Cherry nodded. Midge rolled her eyes and continued.

"The men who followed Cherry are after *this* book. They took my old copy by mistake. That means we've still got what they want. Whatever that is," she wondered, staring at the book in her hand.

"That's good news...isn't it?" Cherry faltered.

Midge shook her head. "It would be, except the kidnappers must think they've got what they wanted. They won't be coming back here any time soon. And they've got Velma."

"Can't we just find these terrible men and give them the book in exchange for Velma?" Tom asked.

"It may not be that simple," Midge said ominously. "You finish in here, Cherry. I'll search downstairs, and Tom, you search my bedroom and the bathroom."

"What are we looking for?" he asked.

"Anything that could lead us to Velma. Anything at all!"

The three split up and for the next ten minutes they turned the tidy house upside down in a frantic attempt to unearth a clue regarding Velma's disappearance.

lowered her voice. "You girls go to San Francisco.
get there, look up my friend, Officer Jackie Jones.
out of the Castro Street station. Make sure to tell
a friend of Betty's. I'll do my best to get in touch
efore you get there, but it may be tough. There's a
ewing in the city, and all the cops have been called
it.

appened?" Cherry asked, fascinated.

ne's snatched a whole convent of nuns," Betty said
he entire order of The Sisters of Mercy has sud-
ppeared!"

why would anyone kidnap nuns?" Cherry slapped
n her forehead. "What's this world coming to?"

bruptly jumped up from the table. "I'll be right
said. But several minutes passed, and Midge hadn't
Cherry looked around the restaurant and spied
ng in the corner. She was on the telephone, but she
king. "She's trying to get in touch with someone,"
ught. "I wonder who?"

ut down the telephone receiver and came back to
'I'm sorry," she said. "Where were you, Betty?"

ust about to say that I can post someone at your
ase anyone shows up or calls, if that's okay with
ge nodded her approval. "We'll keep in touch by
"

to go to San Francisco, too," said Tom, eagerly.

ou have the most important job of all," Midge said,

ghtened. "What's my assignment?"

ob, Tom, is to babysit the kids!"

" exclaimed Monty. "A dog on my beautiful new
et?"

aid Midge. "Six dogs. Six dogs, a cat, one rabbit,
a pig, a bird and a turtle. The mice can take care of
s."

out his head on the table and pretended to cry. Tom
n around his chum and tried to comfort him.
ay. We'll just cover the whole house in plastic. It
t like your mother's!"

lly, could it get any worse?" Monty groaned.

ne laughed, even Monty.

CHAPTER 9

An Important Clue

 Tom came out of the bathroom looking
distressed. "I didn't find any clues,"
he admitted. "Unless this is one," he
said, holding up a pair of sheer
black panties. "Whose could they
be?" he teased.

"They're Velma's—of course!" Midge said, blushing a little. She snatched the panties out of his hand and threw them
on the bureau. She clutched her stomach. "Gosh, I get hungry at the queerest times!" she exclaimed.

"I'm not sure I can continue to hunt for clues on an empty
stomach," Tom chimed in. Suddenly, his eyes lit up. "Speaking of food, I just remembered something. I overheard the men
who took Velma talking about food. I think they were discussing pies, of all things. Now what kind was it?" he mused.

"Apple," guessed Midge.

"Chocolate?" guessed Cherry. "Pecan? That's my favorite."

"No, it was a fruit." Tom thought a minute. "I've got it!"
he cried. "I heard them say something about cherry pie."

"Cherry pie!" Cherry yelped. "They weren't talking about
cherry pie, they were talking about me! That settles it; they
were after me! I just remembered—Velma was wearing my
buttercup-yellow frock! They must have gotten us mixed up!
But who are they?"

"Would it help if we had the license number of the car?"
Tom suggested.

The girls blinked at him with astonishment.

"You have the license number?" Midge cried.

"Well, you know I have this habit of memorizing things for
fun," he said.

"Why didn't you say so sooner?" Cherry admonished.

"I forgot," Tom said apologetically. "I get nervous when
things like this happen."

"And they call females the weaker sex," Midge teased. "Let's have it." Tom closed his eyes, and concentrated. In a moment, he recalled not only the license number of the car, but other details, as well.

"It was a fabulous shiny red convertible with California plates," he recalled. "I wish I had one!"

"Midge says we can't call the police; how will knowing the license number of the car help us? We can't trace it ourselves," Cherry pointed out.

"I know a cop we can trust!" Tom declared. "Midge, remember that uniform party I went to at the Miraloma Club last month?" Midge shook her head. She didn't remember.

"You know," Tom urged. "I borrowed your café curtains for my costume. I went as Lawrence of Arabia."

"I remember now," Midge nodded. "Our curtains never looked so good. He returned them washed and pressed," she told Cherry.

"A uniform party? I could go to one of those," Cherry babbled nervously, remembering the two starched nurse's uniforms tucked securely in her luggage.

"My point is," Tom continued, "at the party there was a girl dressed as a cop who turned out to be the real thing. She said to call her if I ever needed a friend on the force. Her name is Betty. I don't remember her last name, but she's the only girl cop in town, so it shouldn't be too hard to track her down."

While Tom went downstairs to call the police station, Cherry went into the bathroom to powder her nose. Tom returned a few minutes later with good news. "Betty's on her way over," he reported. "She said not to touch anything, but I told her it was too late."

Cherry grimaced as she surveyed the topsy-turvy bedroom. "Nancy Clue would have known not to touch anything," she mused.

For a moment, her thoughts strayed from the drama at hand. It had been only two days since she had read about the murder of Carson Clue, but so much had happened in the meantime, she hadn't had a spare second to think about it. "I've been too busy even to read the newspapers. Golly, I hope Nancy's okay," she thought anxiously. Reluctantly, she put all thoughts about Nancy aside, and set about helping Tom and Midge straighten the room.

While Tom tidied, he whis
"What a festive melody,"
"I don't know," Tom repl
round in my head for the last
title. This happens to me all
crazy!"

"I know the title of that so
Francisco'. It's from that old

Tom shrugged. "I don't kr
my head. I must have heard i
of the men was whistling it.
think they inadvertently gav
must be headed for San Frai

"And we're going to sta
Midge declared. "We're goin

Midge threw some clothes
with the book from Nurse Ma
figure out why this book is s

"Let's get your car gasse
waits for Betty. Meet us at the
Main as soon as you can," sl

Twenty minutes later, Ch
by Tom and Betty, as well a
tween bites of perfectly scra
excitedly explained everythi

Betty sat quietly while ev
did speak, she exuded confic
better already, knowing tha

"The first thing to do is
Velma was taken away in,"

The group perked up.

"But it's probably been st
all that useful to us."

Everyone slumped with d

"The good news is that Ve
care of herself," Midge pipe

"Velma's tough?" asked Cl
woman with the girlish giggle

"The stories I could tell
Cherry.

"We'll have story time lat

plan." Sl
When yo
She worl
her you'r
with her
big case
in to solv

"Wha
"Some
darkly.
denly dis

"Golly
her hand

Midge
back," sl
returned.
Midge pa
wasn't ta
Cherry tl

Midge
the table

"I was
house in
you." Mi
telephone

"I war
"Tom,
solemnly
Tom b
"Your
"What
white ca
"No,"
one guine
themselv

Monty
put his a
"It's o
will be ju
"Oh, g
Every

CHAPTER 10

San Francisco Bound

Midge insisted on driving the first leg of the journey. "I'm too tense to sleep," she said as she took the wheel. Cherry quickly fell asleep in the seat next to her, using Midge's leather jacket as a pillow. When she awoke, Midge was singing along softly to a country western station between puffs on a cigarette. She noticed Cherry was awake and grinned.

"I guess I shouldn't be smoking in front of a nurse. It is a filthy habit."

Cherry said nothing, but opened the window to clear the car.

"I read you," sighed Midge as she stubbed out her cigarette in the already overflowing ashtray. "I only smoke when I'm nervous. Or when Velma's family visits. Or after sex."

Cherry blushed at the confession, making Midge laugh. "You're cute when you blush," she said, making Cherry blush even more.

"You dating anyone?" Midge asked.

"No," Cherry said abruptly.

"Why not?"

"I'm too busy. After all, nursing is an important profession and my job keeps me occupied. It's rewarding and fulfilling work."

"And there's no chance of meeting anyone at work, right?" Midge teased her. "Golly, Cherry, you sound like a nurse recruitment poster! What's a nice girl like you doing all alone?"

Cherry groaned. "You sound just like my mother," she said.

Midge laughed and lit another cigarette. "I bet your mother and I don't have the same thing in mind."

"What did Midge mean?" Cherry wondered. "I just never seem to meet anyone I really like," she said.

It was true. For try as she might, Cherry didn't find the

doctors and interns at her hospital very interesting, despite the attention they paid her.

"You'll meet somebody someday," Midge assured her. "I hooked up with a couple of losers before getting involved with Velma."

"You mean...you and Velma..." Cherry blushed a deep crimson. "Golly! I mean...oh!" she cried, covering her red face with her hands. "Nurse Cassie Case is right. Sometimes I can be so naïve!"

Midge laughed at her consternation. "It's okay, Cherry. Lots of people think we're just roommates, especially since Velma's such a fem."

Cherry blushed some more. Golly, Midge was bold!

"Don't you think Velma's a dish?" Midge wanted to know.

"I don't know if I should say, since we look so much alike," Cherry smiled sheepishly. "She certainly seems like a lovely person."

Cherry found the idea of Midge and Velma as a couple strangely stimulating. "Tell me how you met," she urged.

"Velma." Midge sighed, lit another cigarette, and settled in to tell the story of their romance. "I had been single for a couple of years. Oh, I had a couple of dates here and there, but nothing to write home about. Then one day I was at the library looking up books about hypnosis. I had an idea, well, never mind. It's not important."

"Oh, tell me," Cherry insisted. "Don't leave out a thing."

"I was working on a book about a girl who hypnotizes her parents. I'm a writer." Midge grimaced. "Well, I would be if I could ever finish anything. But that's another story. Anyway, I knocked some books off the stacks, and this really cute girl came over to help me. When I looked up I found myself staring into the greenest eyes I had ever seen. I was completely smitten."

Cherry was transfixed. "A chance encounter—how romantic!" she swooned. "You fell madly in love with each other, and you've lived happily ever after."

Midge laughed. "Not so fast. You've read too many romance novels, Cherry. Our path to love was a little rocky."

"How come?" Cherry asked. "What happened?"

Midge shrugged. "Stuff got in our way. It took us a while, but when we finally did get together, it was well worth the wait." She sighed and rubbed her eyes. "Jeez, I'm tired," she yawned.

"Midge, you look awful. Let's stop at the next diner," Cherry suggested. "A cup of coffee and a snack will invigorate you."

Midge checked her watch and groaned. "There's no time! It's already two a.m. As it is, we're not going to get there until dawn."

"If we have an accident because you're too tired to drive, we won't get there at all. Either stop and get a cup of coffee, or let me drive," Cherry commanded.

Midge pulled off the road and into the parking lot of a small diner. "Let's get it to go," she suggested. While they waited for their order of cheeseburgers and French fries, Midge gulped several cups of coffee. Cherry tried unsuccessfully to contact her aunt.

"Let's go," Midge said, grabbing the sack of food and heading outside. To Cherry's consternation, Midge was halfway through her sandwich by the time they got to the car.

Midge slid behind the wheel and gunned the engine. Cherry hopped inside, spread a handkerchief over her lap and nibbled at her sandwich.

"You're going to get sick," she warned, watching Midge wolf her food as they pulled out of the parking lot and back onto the highway. "You should chew every mouthful thirty times to aid digestion."

"Yes, Nurse Bossy," Midge said, gulping down the last bite of her food.

"I bet you were a real handful as a kid," Cherry teased.

Midge snorted. "Yeah, and I bet you were the real quiet type who always did as you were told," she shot back.

Cherry nodded. "I tried always to obey my elders," she admitted. "I was the kind your type liked to pick on."

"I was a real wiseacre, as my grandmother liked to say, but I was never mean," Midge assured her. "I don't pick on people. Unless it's an ex-girlfriend. Then it's okay."

Cherry laughed. She was really beginning to like Midge, although sometimes she couldn't tell when she was teasing.

"I shouldn't be enjoying myself," Cherry frowned. "Especially not now."

"Everything will be fine," Midge said.

Cherry shook her head. "How can you be so steady at a time like this?" she asked.

Midge just shrugged. "Years of practice," she said vaguely. Cherry waited, but Midge said nothing more. She seemed lost in thought. Cherry wished she knew Midge better. She was dying to know why Midge seemed so upset when Betty told them about the missing nuns. "Is Midge Catholic?" she wondered. Cherry searched for something to say that would bring Midge back to the present.

"You never finished your story," Cherry prompted. "About how you and Velma finally got together."

Midge leaned back in the seat and lit a cigarette. "Where was I? Oh, yeah. One night we made a late date to meet at the library," she said.

Cherry screwed up her nose. "The library doesn't sound very romantic!" she cried.

"Where I'm from it is."

"Where's that?" Cherry asked.

"South," Midge said. "But that's not important."

Cherry was becoming *very* curious about Midge. Was it her imagination, or was Midge a little vague about her background? She put her questions aside as Midge continued her story.

"So one night Velma and I ended up getting locked in the library. I guess the guard, er, the custodian, didn't see us when she locked up for the night. We, ah, talked all night and by dawn we knew we belonged together."

Cherry raised an eyebrow. "You, ah, talked?" Now it was Midge's turn to blush.

"That's all the detail and description I get from Miss Smart Mouth Midge?" Cherry teased.

"C-h-e-r-r-y! Some things are private!"

Cherry laughed. "You're as big a prude as I am!"

"Wel-l-l..." Midge said.

"I have an idea, Midge. Why don't you write about you and Velma?"

"Maybe someday I will, kid," was all Midge would say, but Cherry could tell she was pleased by the suggestion.

Cherry noticed that, despite the stimulants she had consumed, Midge was looking pretty tired. Midge didn't want to stop driving, but Cherry was firm. As a nurse she knew the importance of being fully alert while operating a motor vehicle.

Midge grudgingly pulled off the road and gave up the wheel to Cherry. As soon as she had settled in the passenger seat, she fell fast asleep. Cherry rolled down the window a bit to clear the smoky car and dumped the ashtray full of butts into a little paper bag from the glove box. She was no litter bug!

She covered Midge with the plaid stadium blanket she always kept in the back seat and got ready for the next few lonely hours. For company she turned on the radio, keeping it low so as not to wake Midge.

Cherry pulled out of the parking lot and expertly steered the blue Buick onto the highway.

She fixed her eyes on the road ahead. Little did she know of the adventure in store for her at the end of this long journey!

CHAPTER 11

Follow That Car!

The Golden Gate Bridge glowed magnificently in the pink early-morning light. Cherry nudged Midge awake. "We're here!" she squealed.

Midge sighed and covered her face with her hands. "It's too early to get up, Mom," she groaned sleepily. "Are you always so cheerful first thing in the morning?" she grumbled, squinting at Cherry. "Gosh, I feel awful. Where are we?"

"We're exactly two hundred twenty feet above the Pacific Ocean, Midge, on the Golden Gate Bridge," Cherry answered.

Midge looked troubled. "How far up did you say we were?" She gulped as she peered out her window at the blue expanse of ocean below.

"Don't worry, Midge. There's enough steel wire supporting this bridge to circle the earth three times."

"If you ever give up nursing, you can become a tour guide," Midge laughed. She peered out the window at the giant steel structure, painted burnt orange. "So where's the gold?" she asked.

"You ask a lot of questions, young lady," Cherry said sternly, doing her best Nurse Marstad imitation.

Midge shook her head. "I've heard that before. I've always been like that. Drove my mom crazy." She fumbled through her jacket pockets for a cigarette, but found only empty packages. "Great. First Velma disappears. Now I run out of cigarettes. Could things get any worse?" she joked sourly.

Cherry had some news she hoped would cheer up Midge. "Guess what?" she chirped. "I have some exciting news. I heard on the radio that Nancy Clue is believed to be somewhere in San Francisco, and if the authorities can find her, they're going to call on her to solve the case of the missing nuns! Maybe she could help us, too!"

Midge made a face. "You mean that little rich goody-two-shoes who's always doing some good deed? The one who works with her famous attorney father, Carson Clue? Who solves every mystery without mussing her hair?"

"Haven't you heard, Midge? Don't you know what happened?" Cherry cried.

Cherry related everything she knew about the murder of Carson Clue. "The Clue's loyal housekeeper Hannah Gruel, who had been like a mother to Nancy since the death of her real mother twenty-one years ago, went berserk a few days ago while making a pie and shot Mr. Clue dead!"

Midge didn't seem too upset by the news. "If I had to clean somebody's house and cook his meals for twenty-one years, I'd kill him, too," she said gruffly.

"But Nancy and her father were very close," Cherry explained, a little put off by Midge's flip remark.

"Well that's too bad, then," Midge said, a softer tone creeping into her voice. "I guess I'm not much for family life, outside of me and Velma," she said. "Besides, even if we could find this Nancy Clue girl, we couldn't possibly afford her. Why, she's a rich society dame."

Cherry shook her head. Obviously, Midge wasn't much of a Nancy Clue fan! "She works for free, out of the goodness of her heart. I'm sure she'll help us, she's just got to!"

But Midge wasn't won over. "We'll just have to see about this girl dick," was all she would say.

Cherry smiled. She just knew that despite the tragedy of her own circumstances, Nancy Clue would help them. Her heart raced at the thought of meeting her beloved heroine.

"How about some breakfast," Cherry suggested. She was secretly hoping that if Midge got some food in her stomach, she'd be more agreeable to the idea of contacting Nancy Clue.

"Okay, but first I need to get to a phone and check in with Betty," Midge said anxiously. "I wonder if she's made any progress on the case? I wish they could put telephones in cars. That would sure save us a lot of time."

"I don't know, Midge. I can't see how it would be safe for people to drive and talk on the telephone at the same time," Cherry said. "Midge must be awfully tired to have such a strange idea," Cherry thought. By this time they were in a part of the city with hills so steep it felt like they were on a carnival ride.

"This area is called Russian Hill. Look, Midge, a cable car! Did you know that by the turn of the century San Francisco had six hundred cable cars traveling over one hundred miles of track?"

Cherry's command of details astonished her passenger. "How on earth did you know that?" Midge asked.

"After I decided to visit my Aunt Gertrude, I wrote to the San Francisco Chamber of Commerce and got pertinent information," Cherry replied. "In my glove box, I've got a notebook containing all kinds of information, like temperatures, average price of a meal, and things to see. And I know the safest parts of the city, just in case there's an earthquake."

If such an emergency did occur, Cherry was fully prepared, with fresh uniforms and a medical kit securely stowed in her trunk.

"Cherry, you're beginning to remind me of my favorite Girl Scout leader, Miss Mary Metz, a woman who could pull just about anything out of her purse," Midge chuckled.

That was high praise indeed, coming from Midge!

"In another few blocks, we'll be in the Castro area," Cherry said happily. "I stopped at a service station a few hours ago, filled the tank and purchased a map. You slept through the whole thing. Rather, you snored through the whole thing."

"No one's ever complained before," Midge said.

"Have a lot of girls had the opportunity to hear you snore?" Cherry teased.

Midge blushed, and changed the subject. "I think we're in the Castro," she announced. "Hey, look, there's the police station!"

They were lucky enough to find a parking spot right in front. "How convenient!" Cherry cried. "Maybe our luck is changing."

Midge slunk down in her seat and pulled her jacket collar high above her ears. "Cherry, why don't you go in and ask for Officer Jones? I'll stay out here with the car."

Cherry was frankly puzzled by Midge's strange behavior. She was just about to tease Midge about being shy, when she remembered her earlier reluctance to call the police. "There's something she's not telling me," Cherry decided. "I wonder what it is?"

She hopped out of the car, but not before taking a quick look in the rear view mirror to make sure she was presentable.

"Golly, I look tired," she groaned when saw the dark circles under her eyes. She reached for her compact.

"Cherry, let's make this a quick visit," Midge said nervously. "Didn't you say something about breakfast? And you still haven't gotten in touch with your aunt. Besides, you look fine. Really great. Never looked better."

Cherry knew she didn't look her best, but she didn't want to upset Midge any further. "I'll hurry," she said, racing out of the car and up the stairs. Once inside, Cherry looked around in confusion. The noise was deafening. Everywhere, people were talking and telephones were ringing. "Where do I go?" she wondered. She had never been in that kind of place before. "It's kind of scary in here," she thought. "I wish Midge had come with me. What if I run into a real live criminal?"

She walked up to a big, tall girl outfitted in a peach chiffon cocktail dress with a matching bolero jacket. "Excuse me, where would I go to find a particular officer?" she asked, adding, "By the way, I love your gown."

"Thanks. I made it myself," the girl replied, in a startlingly deep voice. "The front desk is right over there," she said, waving her cream-colored elbow-length gloves towards the back of the room.

Cherry thanked the friendly girl. "My, that was an unusually dressy outfit for this early in the morning," she thought, as she made her way to the front desk. "And, although she was very attractive, I'd do something about that mustache."

"Excuse me. I'm looking for Officer Jones," she said to the burly cop sitting behind the desk.

"Her shift doesn't begin for an hour. Come back then." He turned his back and began to type furiously.

"Do you know where I can find her now?" Cherry pressed. "It's really important," she added.

He stopped typing, and glared at Cherry. "I said, come back in an hour."

"Golly, he was uncooperative," she thought as she left, her face flushed with anger. "Why, if I weren't in such a hurry, I'd speak to his superior about his attitude!"

She spied a telephone booth in the corner of the lobby. "As long as I'm here, I might as well call Aunt Gert and tell her I'm in town," Cherry decided. She let the telephone ring for a very long time, thinking that her aunt might be out in her back yard, pruning her fruit trees.

But Aunt Gert never came to the phone. "That's odd!" she cried. "This is the third time I've called and gotten no answer. Aunt Gert knows I'm scheduled to arrive today. She hasn't been home for days. How odd!"

She raced outside and found Midge leaning against the car, looking around frantically. "I'm so relieved to see you!" Midge cried. "I was afraid something happened in there. Did you find Officer Jones?"

Cherry shook her head. "Her shift doesn't start for another forty-five minutes. We'll have to come back then."

"We can't wait any longer!" Midge cried. "Velma's already been missing for twelve hours. We're losing valuable time. We need to find Officer Jones now!"

Someone tapped Cherry on the shoulder. Why, it was the big-boned girl in the beautiful chiffon dress Cherry had met inside.

"I hope you don't think I'm nosy, but I couldn't help over-hearing your friend," the stranger said. "I know Officer Jones. She usually has coffee at Flora's Café in the mornings. You could try there.

"It's right around the corner," she added helpfully. "It's the place with all the dogs waiting out front."

"Thank you!" Cherry cried gratefully. "You've been a big help."

"Oh, sure, honey," the girl said, waving good-bye.

Midge grabbed Cherry's hand, and they raced to the cof-fee shop. The place was packed with people drinking coffee and chatting in a leisurely fashion. "They look like they have all the time in the world," said Cherry, thinking about her hectic life as a nurse in a big-city hospital. "Don't these peo-ple work?"

Midge suggested that since San Francisco was a drop-off point for the military after the war, there were probably a lot of retired soldiers with time on their hands. "And lots of WACs," she said, elbowing Cherry. "How do you feel about girls in uniform?"

"All that's on my mind right now is finding Officer Jones," Cherry replied, blushing nonetheless. Secretly, she did think girls in uniform looked *quite* dashing!

"That darn Midge can practically read my mind," Cherry thought.

Midge looked around. "I don't see any police officers," she said.

Cherry pointed out a stocky girl clad in blue serge slacks and shirt and heavy leather boots. What really caught Cherry's eye were the handcuffs hanging from the girl's belt. "That must be Officer Jones!" she exclaimed triumphantly. Before Midge could stop her, Cherry rushed up to the girl.

"I'm a friend of Betty's!" she cried.

The girl grinned and raised one eyebrow. "My, my, my," she said, looking Cherry up and down and smiling. "I'm a friend of Betty's too. What's your name?"

Cherry felt a tug at her elbow. It was Midge. "Ixnay, Cherry. You've got the wrong girl," Midge whispered in her ear.

"But...but..." Cherry cried. Midge pulled her over to a table and deposited her in a chair.

"Don't talk to anyone. I'll be right back," she said.

A moment later, Midge returned carrying two cups of steaming coffee and a plate of breakfast rolls.

"I don't understand!" Cherry cried.

"I know, Cherry," Midge laughed.

A red-haired girl at the adjoining table shushed them. She went back to scribbling furiously in her notebook.

"Mind if we *sit* here?" Midge asked sarcastically.

The girl took a few seconds to answer. She did not appear to be in the best of moods, Cherry noticed.

"I don't care what you do, as long as you do it quietly," she hissed.

"Must be one of those nutty San Francisco writers you're always hearing about," Midge whispered to Cherry. "You know, they sit all day drinking coffee and writing. They don't work or anything. No one has any idea how they live."

"Shhh," Cherry whispered. "She might hear you. I'd feel more comfortable sitting outside. Besides, it's a lovely morning."

They took their coffee and rolls to the front stoop. Cherry settled near a gray and white Sheltie with sky-blue eyes. The dog put her head on Cherry's arm and sighed.

"What's wrong, sweetie?" asked Cherry, breaking off a piece of her roll for the dog. The dog daintily ate the offering and licked Cherry's hand in appreciation. Midge shared her roll with a Pekinese, who was doing tricks for her breakfast.

Midge sighed. "I miss my pets. I miss my girlfriend."

Suddenly someone appeared on the steps behind them. It was the crabby writer. "Too loud?" Midge asked, in a rude manner. Cherry hoped Midge wasn't going to start a fight! She held her breath.

The girl looked chagrined. "I'm a big grouch when I have a deadline," she said in an apologetic way.

Midge looked remorseful. The girl knelt and patted the little blue-eyed dog. "I see you've met Princess," she said.

"She's a beauty," chorused Midge and Cherry.

"Time to go home," the girl said, bending down to unleash her pet. The dog licked her on her nose and off they went.

"Well, there goes a happy couple," Midge said. "Too bad she was so grouchy. She was kind of cute, don't you think, Cherry?"

Cherry blushed and changed the subject quickly. "It must be time to go back to the police station," she said primly, making a big show of checking her watch. "In fact, we should have been there three whole minutes ago," she gasped.

"You go without me," Midge said. "I'll try to get in touch with Betty. Meet me back here."

Cherry raced to the police station and was sorely disappointed to learn that Officer Jones had already been sent out on assignment. "You're welcome to wait, lady," the sergeant said, pointing to a wooden bench already overflowing with impatient people. "But I don't know when she's going to be back."

"No, thanks," Cherry sighed. She persuaded the officer to let her leave a note and walked dejectedly back to the coffee shop. When she got there, Midge was sitting on the front steps, nursing her cup of coffee and looking pretty discouraged.

"Hey," Midge sighed upon spying Cherry. "I can tell you didn't find Officer Jones; it's written all over your face."

"I left a note telling her what we look like and where we're parked. Any luck getting in touch with Betty?" Cherry asked.

Midge shook her head. "I called, but she's out on a case. Our best chance of finding the men who have Velma is to find their car. To do that, we need a cop." Midge shuddered.

Cherry sat on the steps next to Midge. "I called my aunt, but she's not home either. What do we do next?" she asked, but stopped short when she realized she was talking to thin air.

For Midge was bounding up the block and yelling Velma's name!

Cherry panted as she raced up the steep hill behind her.

"I just saw a red convertible speed by," Midge yelled over her shoulder. "And Velma was in the back seat!"

Cherry was grateful she had selected flats as her travel shoes, otherwise she would have never been able to keep up with Midge as she raced up the steep Castro Street hill.

"Quick! Let's go back and get the car. If we hurry, we might be able to catch them!" Midge cried. She took off back down the hill with Cherry close behind her.

But when they reached Cherry's car, a police officer blocked their way. "What's going on?" Cherry cried.

"We're impounding a stolen car, miss," the officer replied in a peremptory manner.

"But that's *my* car," she asserted.

"Can you prove it?" asked the police officer.

Cherry went to the glove box and found it wide open. "That's odd," she said. "I distinctly remember having shut this." A closer inspection revealed that someone had tampered with it. Cherry's registration, title and pad of paper containing all her San Francisco information were gone!

Cherry looked under the floor mat and between the seats, but her search was futile. "Someone's stolen my registration!" she cried.

"Something's been stolen, all right, and I think I'm looking at the thieves!" said the police officer, glaring at Cherry and Midge. "Come with me, girls. You're under arrest!"

Midge, who was usually quick to fly off the handle, remained surprisingly calm. "But officer," she said, her voice as sweet as pie, "surely you don't think *we're* thieves." Was it Cherry's imagination, or did she just catch Midge batting her eyelashes?

"We're nurses...er, Girl Scout nurses, in San Francisco to attend a Girl Scout Jamboree and teach first-aid techniques."

Cherry was speechless at Midge's sudden fabrication.

"Well," said the cop, looking skeptical. "Can you prove it?"

"Er...ah..." Midge fudged for time. Cherry's mind raced. Suddenly, she had it.

"Our nurse's uniforms are in the trunk of our car—check for yourself!" she cried. Phew!

The police officer agreed to check the trunk. He first opened Midge's bag. Cherry puzzled over the pair of handcuffs he found.

"Oh, those are for a life-saving technique," said Midge, pocketing the cuffs. "We keep our uniforms in there," she said, pointing to Cherry's white leather suitcase.

Indeed, inside the bag were two freshly-starched nurse's uniforms and two matching caps. Two pairs of freshly polished white shoes were tucked in a shoe bag in the bottom of the suitcase.

"Well, it certainly looks like you're nurses," said a cop, a grin breaking over his burly face. "Say, my daughter's a Girl Scout—where did you say your jamboree was?"

Cherry, who wasn't even sure what a jamboree was, kept her mouth shut. This time Midge groped for an answer.

"Uh...uh..."

"Causing more trouble, huh, girls?" It was the grouchy writer from the coffee shop, and her little dog, too.

"What's wrong, officer; what did these two do?" the girl asked.

"You know these girls?" he asked.

The writer grinned. "Sure I do; we're old pals."

"And they're Girl Scouts?"

"Absolutely."

Then the girl did a very queer thing. She put down her book bag and sang a song to the tune of "Frère Jacques"; a little off-key but charming, nonetheless:

I'm a Girl Scout; I'm a Girl Scout.
Who are you? Who are you?
Can't you tell by looking? Can't you tell by looking?
I'm one, too. I'm one, too!

There was applause all around, even from passersby.

The police officer looked chagrined. "Well, girls, I guess the stolen auto report was a prank. Sorry to have bothered you." He tipped his hat and strolled away.

"But wait!" Cherry cried. "Someone has stolen my car papers." But she was too late, for the police officer had already ducked into a nearby donut shop.

"Velma's kidnappers have a lot of nerve reporting us to the police as car thieves," Midge snarled. She clenched her fists. "If I could just get my hands on them! By now, I'm sure they're miles away from here. I guess we're stuck here until Officer Jones arrives. When we do find her, we'll insist she immediately run a check on the license number of the car!" Midge fumbled through her jacket pockets. "Jeez, I wish I had a cigarette."

She found a butt on the floor of the car and lit it. Cherry examined herself in the car window. "I'm so rumpled," she wailed. She look at her wrinkled outfit with dismay. "If only Aunt Gert were home, we could at least have a place to freshen up. I'd sure love to change my clothes," she wished aloud.

"Actually, Cherry, this *would* be a good time for you to change your clothes," Midge agreed. She crushed the cigarette under her black penny loafers. "Follow me!"

"What is she up to?" Cherry wondered. Midge didn't strike her as the type to worry about anyone's appearance, especially in the middle of a mystery!

"Where are we going?" Cherry asked as she walked behind Midge. "Does it involve running?" Cherry groaned. "It does, doesn't it?"

CHAPTER 12

A New Identity

"If I'm going to change my clothes, shouldn't I have my suitcase?" Cherry asked.

"Cherry, I had a terrible realization back there. If those thugs see you, they'll know they've got the wrong girl and then they might come after you. Why, they might even harm Velma if they think she's of no use to them!" Midge added.

Cherry gasped. "What a horrible thought!" she cried. "We've got to do something."

Midge nodded. "I think the best way to protect both you and Velma is to disguise you somehow."

"I could tie a scarf over my head and get some dark glasses," Cherry said.

Midge shook her head. "You'll just look like someone who's trying to hide," she said. "We need to make you look so different that even your own mother wouldn't recognize you."

Midge pushed Cherry through the doorway of Mr. Harold's House of Hair. Cherry had a funny feeling something very queer was about to happen.

"What can I do for you girls?" asked a man in a crisp baby-blue smock.

"My friend needs a haircut," Midge said. "And we're in a bit of a hurry."

"I'll see if Mr. Harold is available," he said politely, disappearing through flowered curtains in the back of the room. He returned a moment later. "You're in luck," he smiled. "There's been a cancellation. Mr. Harold can see you right now."

Cherry wasn't so sure how lucky she felt, but she didn't say anything as the man guided her to a salon chair and tied the strings of a plastic smock around her neck.

"Midge, you won't let him do anything really awful to me, will you?" she begged.

Midge patted Cherry on the shoulder. "Just trust me," she said. "I know what looks good on a girl."

A moment later Mr. Harold came sailing though the curtains. He glided over to Cherry, took a comb from his smock pocket, and ran it through her mop of tousled curls.

"Tsk, tsk. Who gave you this cut, dear?"

Cherry gulped. "I had it cut in Idaho last year," she said. "My mother's friend Lucille does hair in her basement..." She stopped when she realized the man wasn't listening. He was staring intently at her head and frowning. Cherry squirmed under the hot plastic smock. She was beginning to feel like a specimen under a microscope.

"This is an awfully outdated look for such a young girl," Mr. Harold proclaimed. "If I were you, I'd go with a sportier look." He pulled Cherry's thick dark hair off her face and secured it with several bobby pins. He stepped back a few feet and frowned.

"What do you think, Roberto?"

The man in the baby-blue smock agreed that Cherry's hair needed a dramatic change.

"What did you have in mind, dear?" Mr. Harold asked. Cherry was about to say that she didn't have a thing in mind, when she realized the hairdresser was speaking to Midge!

Midge whispered something in Mr. Harold's ear—something Cherry couldn't hear.

He nodded. "I know what you want," he said.

Mr. Harold took a large pair of shears from the drawer of a pink plastic vanity table, and soon locks of her dark curly hair fell to the floor.

Cherry closed her eyes and screwed up her courage. "I'm doing this for the safety of everyone concerned," she told herself.

It was hard to keep from crying when she heard the buzz of the clippers on her neck. "Oh, what will Mother say?" she wondered.

A few minutes later, the buzzing stopped. "It's a new you," Mr. Harold announced grandly, as he twirled the chair around so she was facing the mirror.

"Open your eyes, dear," he chuckled. "It's over."

"I'm scared!" Cherry cried. "Why, I can feel the air on the

back of my neck!" she wailed. She peeked at her reflection.

"Eek!" she cried, upon spying the cap of short curly hair. "There can't be more than three inches of hair anywhere on my head!" She tugged at her short pixie bangs.

"What is Nurse Marstad going to say?" she cried. "Regulations state I've got to have enough hair to pin my cap on," she explained. "And my mother..."

Cherry stopped. Why, she didn't even want to think about what her mother was going to say when she saw her new hair-do!

"I look like a boy!" she wailed.

Midge chuckled. "Cherry, no one could ever mistake you for a boy. Well, not yet, anyway." She evaluated Cherry's new hair-do with a critical eye.

"That's better," she said. "Now all you need are some new clothes."

"A new outfit *would* cheer me up," Cherry said, glumly surveying her new short hair-do. "How fast does hair grow?" she wondered.

Midge paid Mr. Harold and purchased a small can of hair pomade. She slipped a dollar into his hand.

"Stop fussing with your hair," she said to Cherry. "Let's go."

Cherry walked a few paces behind Midge, pausing now and then to get a glimpse of herself in store windows. "What did you buy back there?" she asked.

"You'll find out," Midge said mysteriously.

"You're always saying that," Cherry complained. "Why, Midge, I..." But before she could finish, Midge hurried her into a store. "See that cop car out there?" Midge asked, pointing to a patrol car cruising slowly down the street. "This is the third time I've spotted that car going up and down this block."

"Maybe it's that friend of Betty's," Cherry suggested eagerly.

"And maybe our pals in the red convertible have made another false report on us," Midge replied bitterly. "We'd better lay low until we complete your makeover."

"But if I change the way I look, how will Betty's friend recognize us?" Cherry asked. "In my note, I told her to look for a tall blond girl in jeans and a dark-haired girl wearing a pink seersucker shift."

"She'll know it's us," Midge said.

Cherry sighed. "You'll explain later, right?"

Midge grinned. "Right. Now let's get you some clothes."

Cherry exclaimed over the pretty dresses she saw as they walked through the large department store. "It's time I got a few new things," she thought.

As much as she enjoyed wearing her nurse's whites, especially the cute cap and dashing cape, she did get tired of appearing in the same outfit over and over again. And, as her mother had been quick to point out the other day, the white uniform did little to highlight her fair coloring.

Besides, she was beginning to feel a little dowdy in the sleeveless seersucker shift she had thrown on at a rest stop. It had been considered the height of fashion when she bought it last summer in Pleasantville. She noticed that there were many girls dressed like Midge in simple jeans, T-shirts and aviator jackets.

"And all the girls wearing dresses look more high-fashion than I do," she noticed. She pulled a white satin cocktail dress with a beaded bodice off the rack and held it in front of herself.

"What do you think, Midge? Do I look more glamorous?"

Midge made her put the dress back.

"I have something a little different in mind for you," she said. She made a bee-line for the men's department.

She rifled through a display of men's casual slacks. "What size pants do you wear?" she asked.

Cherry was speechless.

"What's the matter, Cherry? Don't girls wear pants in Happy Town, or wherever it is you're from?"

"Pleasantville. But we only wear slacks for gardening. My mother says slacks aren't very feminine."

"They're not—that's the point." Midge held a pair of brown slacks to Cherry's waist. "These look like they'll fit," she said.

A salesman sporting a pencil-thin mustache and an arrogant attitude approached the two girls.

"Are you ladies finding everything you need?" he sniffed.

Midge looked annoyed. "We're fine," she said, turning her back on the man to examine a rack of white button-down shirts.

"Are you looking for anything special today? Perhaps a gift for a special boyfriend?" he persisted.

"Yes, that's it," Midge answered, looking at thin leather belts displayed next to the cash register. Cherry could tell by the tone in her voice that Midge was annoyed.

"Those slacks you picked are some of our finest in men's casual wear," the man said. "They're wash-n-wear and never need ironing. You'll appreciate that," he chuckled.

"I couldn't be happier," Midge replied sarcastically. "Wrap 'em up," she said.

"If you don't mind me saying so, your boyfriend's a pretty small fellow," the man observed, as he rang up Midge's purchases. He stared at Cherry, who was busy examining her new hair-do in the three-way mirror. "Yes, sir, he must be an awfully small fellow for a tall gal like yourself."

"Yeah, he's about your size," Midge retorted. She quickly paid the bill and grabbed Cherry's arm. They sailed through Misses Dresses and ducked into a changing room.

Midge handed the bag of men's clothes to Cherry. "Put these on," she said. "I'll run to the shoe department and get you some shoes. I'd say you were about a size nine." She pulled the curtain tight. "Don't let anyone in," she said.

"But, Midge, if you wanted me to wear slacks, there's a darling pair of capri pants out there," Cherry wailed. But Midge had already left.

Cherry looked with trepidation at the masculine clothes. She kicked off her flats and gingerly slipped on the fly-front baggy slacks. She had just finished buttoning the shirt when Midge stuck her arm through the part in the curtain.

"Here are your shoes," she said, dropping a pair of men's size-seven black penny loafers on the floor. "Let's see how you look."

Cherry poked her head through the curtain and looked around shyly. "There's nobody here," Midge assured her. "Besides, you're going to have to come out sooner or later."

"You look cute," Midge exclaimed as Cherry emerged from the dressing room.

"My mother would die if she could see me," Cherry fretted, putting her hands on her hips in a girlish manner.

"If you're going to wear that outfit, you can't put your hands on your hips like that," Midge said. "Put them in your pockets like I do.

"And when you walk, don't glide or skip or mince. You

have a brother, don't you?" Cherry nodded. "Then walk the way he walks," Midge said.

When Cherry imitated her brother's walk, Midge hooted with laughter. "Forget that," she said. "Watch me."

Midge strode confidently up and down the carpeted hallway outside the dressing room.

Cherry put her hands deep in her pants pockets and imitated Midge's walk.

"That's better," Midge said. "Now, roll up your shirt sleeves."

Then Midge knelt and rolled the cuff of Cherry's trousers. "That'll do for now. Maybe your mom will peg them later," she teased. "That's how butches wear theirs."

She stood back and surveyed her work. "There's just one more thing," she said, reaching in her pocket and taking out the can of pomade she had purchased from Mr. Harold.

"This," she said, "is Butch Wax." She scooped out a dollop of the thick yellow grease, rubbed it between her hands and slicked Cherry's hair off her forehead.

"I was just getting used to it," Cherry cried, as she watched her modern short haircut become a greasy, slicked-back hair-do.

"It will wash out," Midge assured her. "Eventually." She rolled Cherry's old clothes into a bundle and shoved them into the shopping bag. "Put your purse in here," she said. "No self-respecting butch would ever been seen with a purse."

"But where will I keep my lipstick?" Cherry gasped. "And who is this Butch person you're always talking about?" she asked as she followed Midge out of the store.

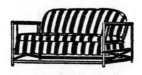

CHAPTER 13

Startling News

It was only noon, but to Cherry and Midge, who had only had a few restless hours sleep the night before, it felt like midnight. "I need some caffeine and sugar, and fast," Midge declared as she staggered down the street.

"No you don't," Cherry said. "What you need is sleep." Nurse Cherry Aimless took charge. "If Officer Jones is not waiting for us when we get back to the car, I'll call Aunt Gert. And if she's not home, we'll check into a motel and freshen up," she declared, taking hold of Midge and directing her back to the car.

"A short nap and a shower do more to combat fatigue than an artificial stimulant," she quoted from her nurse's manual.

There was no note on their car from Officer Jones. "You wait here, Midge," Cherry said. "I'll go look for her again. I'll be right back."

"No problem," the sleepy girl replied. She crawled into the wide back seat of the Buick and fell fast asleep.

For the third time that morning, Cherry found herself inside the Castro Street police station. She got in the line at the front desk, and waited patiently. While she did, she practiced standing with her hands in her pockets, and not on her hips.

She struck up a conversation with an elderly woman in line behind her, who was dressed entirely in white and carrying a small fluffy dog. After a friendly conversation about poodles, the woman startled her by asking her if she'd like to meet her granddaughter.

"Er, no thanks," Cherry replied politely. "I'm only in town a little while and all my time will be taken up visiting my aunt," she added, not wishing to offend the nice woman.

Cherry was relieved when it was her turn to approach the desk.

"Say good-bye to the nice boy, Fluffy," the woman said, waving one of her dog's paws. "Bye, bye."

"Bye," Cherry replied, blushing to the roots of her slicked-back hair.

The officer at the desk stared at Cherry in the most peculiar way. "Wasn't your sister in earlier?" he asked.

"Yes," Cherry said, taking care to lower her voice an octave.

"Officer Jones is not in. Next."

A quick stop at the phone booth revealed Aunt Gert still wasn't home. "Where is everyone?" Cherry wondered.

She raced back to the car. "I can't find anyone, Midge. What are we going to do? What if we don't find her, Midge? Can we call in Nancy Clue then? Midge, are you listening?" She realized that Midge was fast asleep. "And she is *too* snoring," Cherry thought, making a mental note to tease Midge about it later.

She plopped down into the passenger seat and slipped off her new penny loafers, which were giving her blisters. She had walked a lot that day, and most of it uphill. She felt very sleepy herself.

Cherry was a pro at taking short naps. As a student nurse she had often worked double shifts, grabbing a quick nap during her ten minute breaks. After months of this grueling schedule, she was so adept at nodding off that she could fall asleep standing up. Why, once she had even fallen asleep while a doctor was talking to her!

Cherry was far too professional to fall asleep during a patient conference, but this doctor was going on and on about his new motorboat, and Cherry just couldn't stay awake. The incident had earned her the nickname "Sleepy" amongst the doctors, and admiration from the nurses, many of whom had had a similar desire to fall asleep while listening to this particular doctor.

"Maybe I'll just close my eyes for a minute," she thought. Within seconds she was fast asleep.

Cherry was jarred out of a deep sleep by someone knocking at her car window. She opened her eyes and found she was eye-level with a police officer's wide leather belt. "Jeepers," Cherry thought. "I've never seen a gun up close before."

Midge stirred in the back seat. "Cherry, get rid of him," Midge whispered groggily. "Use the Girl Scout nurse story again."

Cherry rolled down her window and pasted a big smile on her face.

"We'll be out of here in just a minute, officer," she said politely.

The police officer leaned down and looked into the car. Midge sat up when she saw the face of a *girl*—a handsome girl with warm brown skin and dancing black eyes.

"Are you by any chance a friend of Betty's?" Cherry asked, staring straight into the girl's deep-set eyes.

A wide, warm grin broke over the officer's face. "I'm Officer Jackie Jones. Call me Jackie." She took off her hat and ran a hand over her short slicked-back hair which glistened blue-black in the sunlight.

Cherry noticed that the girl's short hair-do made her strong jaw even more prominent.

"I'd feel safe with her anywhere," she sighed. Although the sun was shining, Cherry was aware of shivers running down her spine.

Officer Jones leaned one muscular arm on the car window. "You must be Midge," she said, reading from a piece of paper she had taken from her pocket. "Look for a tall blond girl in a leather coat, the note says."

She stared at Cherry.

Cherry melted under the officer's steady gaze.

"You must be Cherry, but you certainly don't fit the description you left me."

"A lot's happened since we got here this morning," Cherry squeaked.

Jackie laughed. "I've heard that story before," she said. "I'm sorry it's taken me so long to find you two. I've been out all morning chasing down a dead-end lead in the missing nuns case. We're all working overtime to find the creeps who have done this," she shuddered.

"How much has Betty told you about our situation?" Midge wanted to know.

"My communication with her was brief," Jackie said. "It's not safe for us to talk at work, and I've been pulling double shifts in this missing nuns case. She told me your girl got snatched. That's pretty rough," she said sadly.

"We saw the car my girlfriend was taken away in. I wasn't able to catch it, but we do have the license number," Midge said.

She filled Jackie in on the strange events of the last few

days, beginning with the disappearance of Cherry's amnesia patient, Lana.

"There's some connection between Lana's disappearance and the kidnapping of my girlfriend," Midge added. She took Lana's book from her jacket pocket and showed it to Jackie. "This is what those thugs are after," she said. "But I haven't been able to figure out why."

"That book must be the link!" Cherry cried. She blushed when she saw the amused look on Midge's face. "You've known it all along, haven't you?" she said. "I am a terrible detective!"

"Cherry worships detectives, especially a particular one named Nancy Clue," Midge grinned. "She even wants to call her in to solve our case."

"Cherry's not the only one who'd like to get her hands on Nancy Clue," Jackie admitted. "Frankly, this missing nuns case has us all stumped. One day there are seventeen nuns going about their quiet lives at the convent of The Sisters of Mercy, and the next, they're all gone. Why, it's as if they've vanished off the face of the earth.

"Nancy's famous for her ability to solve really difficult cases. Even the guys on the force who won't give me the time of day because I'm a female would be happy to see *that* girl right now."

Officer Jones looked at her watch. "I'll check in with the sarge and pretend to shuffle a few papers while I run a check on the license number you gave me, Midge. I can be through within the hour."

When Cherry expressed a keen interest in a bath, Officer Jones directed them to a women's boarding house nearby. "It's inexpensive, but clean," she reported. "I'll meet you there."

"Gee, she's nice," said Cherry, as she and Midge drove in the direction of the rooming house.

"Yeah, and she thinks you're cute, too. Notice the way she looked at you?" Midge teased Cherry.

Cherry blushed, for the trillionth time in her life. Luckily, it was getting dark.

They arrived at the rooming house within minutes. A pleasant woman wearing snug gold capri slacks and a purple knit shell welcomed them to Mary Worth Hall.

"All I've got left is a room with a double bed," she said.

"We'll take it," Midge replied.

"Sign here, girls," the woman said, pushing the register toward them. "That will be six dollars, in advance."

She gave them the key for room 319, along with the bad news that the elevator was broken and it was the bellhop's night off.

"Oh, and there are no men allowed on the premises, this being a girl's hotel and all."

"No problem," Midge said.

"Didn't think so," the woman replied. She winked at Midge, who returned the wink.

"I love San Francisco," Midge whispered to Cherry as they headed for the stairs, bags in hand. The woman bade them a good night, and invited them to come by her room for tea in the morning.

"All the girls do," she said. "Room 7. I'm Betty, by the way."

"Gee, there sure are a lot of Bettys in the world," Cherry said.

"Sure are," Midge grinned.

It had been a long day, and the three flights of stairs didn't help any. Cherry was happy to get to their room. Why, her bags felt as if they contained rocks. "Why did I pack so many outfits?" she groaned.

She threw herself on the bed and sighed deeply. "I've never been more tired," she declared.

"You'll feel better after a little nap," Midge said.

Midge bounced on the bed. "I haven't slept with another girl since the day I met Velma," she kidded.

Cherry jumped up. "I must unpack!" she cried nervously. She opened her suitcase and hung up her uniforms. In case she was pressed into professional service, she certainly wanted to look her best!

"What I need right now more than anything in the world is a hot bath," she declared.

Cherry opened the door to what she thought was the bathroom and was surprised to find a fold-out ironing board instead. She was puzzled. "So where's the bathroom?" she wondered aloud.

"Down the hall, princess," teased Midge, dumping the contents of her valise onto a chair.

Cherry was embarrassed. She had never been to a hotel without a private bathroom before. "But I didn't bring any-

thing to sleep in," she complained. "I left my nightie in Idaho;
I was going to borrow one of Aunt Gert's. Why, I'll have to
wear my slip to bed."

"You worry too much about the way you look. I'm sure the
girls down the hall will think you're cute in any old thing you
wear."

"What do you wear to bed?" asked Cherry.

Midge held up a pair of red plaid boxer shorts.

"Oh, those are cute," Cherry said. "But what do you wear
on top?"

"On top? Do people wear pajama tops, too?" Midge teased.

Cherry assumed Midge was kidding. Or was she? Before she
could ask, there was a knock at the door. Cherry opened it, expecting to find Jackie, but instead there stood a curly-haired
girl clad in satin lounging pajamas. She introduced herself as
Sally and invited them over for popcorn and gin rummy.

"Or, a game of Old Maid, if you like," she added.

Jackie appeared behind Sally, carrying a large paper sack,
which gave off the most wonderful aromas. "I thought you
two might be hungry," she said to Cherry and Midge.

Sally squealed with delight. "How do I get you to deliver
to *my* room?" she asked, coyly giving Jackie's bicep a little
squeeze. Even the usually unflappable Midge blushed.

Jackie just rolled her eyes and pushed past her into the
room. "Get rid of the uniform queen," she whispered to Cherry.

Cherry thanked Sally for her generous invitation, and
diplomatically explained that they had other plans for the
evening.

Sally pouted for a moment and then gave up with a shrug.
"See you at tea," she called cheerfully over her shoulder. Mo-
ments later they heard her knocking at another door, and the
three girls were finally alone to discuss their case.

Jackie locked the door. "Let's have no more interruptions,"
she said, opening the sacks to reveal steaming containers of
Chinese food. The girls eagerly dug into the chow mein, sweet
and sour pork, and other goodies. They ate for a while, sa-
voring the fragrant food.

"I have good news," Jackie announced, after a few bites of
fried prawns. "I was able to trace the car."

Cherry was frankly relieved to be getting some professional
help!

"It belongs to..." she flipped open her note pad for the address. "It belongs to a Miss Gertrude Aimless, 33 Lindy Lane. Isn't that funny, Cherry. She has the same last name as you."

"That's because she's my Aunt Gertrude!" Cherry gasped, almost choking on a won ton. "And although she knows I'm coming for a visit, she hasn't answered her phone for days!"

A concerned look crossed Jackie's face. "It looks like her car was stolen and used in the commission of a crime," she said. "I sent a buddy out to her address to check things out. She should be calling at any minute."

"I just know something terrible has happened to Aunt Gert," Cherry cried. "Please don't take this personally, Jackie, but I think we should alert the entire police force. Why, can't we call in the FBI?"

"I don't think the boys downtown can do any more than what we're already doing. Besides, everyone's assigned to the big missing nuns case. They're not going to be too worried about someone's missing aunt."

Cherry paced nervously around the room. "What do we do now?" she cried.

"I put an APB out on the car, but it's probably been abandoned by now," Jackie said. She put more food on Cherry's plate, but the girl was too worked up to eat.

"I'll eat it," Midge volunteered. "It's nerves. I always eat when I'm upset."

There was a knock at the door. It was Sally. "Telephone for Officer Jones," she said brightly.

"Thanks," Jackie said.

"Sally. That's my name."

"Well, thanks, Sally," Jackie said, this time smiling a little as she brushed past the girl.

Sally lingered in the doorway. "So, you're visiting?"

"Yes," Midge said, obviously reluctant to engage in conversation with a stranger.

"You staying long?"

"Hope not."

Midge said nothing more, yet the girl wouldn't leave. "Who's your friend?" she asked, pointing down the hallway in Jackie's direction.

Midge was thoroughly annoyed. "Look..."

"Sally."

"Look, Sally, we'd really like to be alone right now."

"Oh! The three of you..." Sally voice trailed off. Her eyes lit up. "Oh, I get it. You don't have to draw me a picture...well, unless you really want to, that is," she giggled. "Ta, ta," she sang, flouncing down the hallway.

"Well, she finally got the message," Cherry said, relieved.

Midge rolled her eyes. "I'm not sure it was the right message, but at least she's gone."

The girls heard Sally laughing from the hallway.

"If I'm in trouble, will you rescue me?" they heard her coo.

"What's keeping Jackie?" Cherry wondered. "Perhaps I'd better go and get her." She headed determinedly for the hallway. Just then, Jackie sauntered back into the room, stuffing a piece of paper into her breast pocket and grinning.

"Good going," Midge grinned. "Now who called?"

"A pal of mine talked with Gertrude Aimless a week ago, and she was all excited about Cherry's visit. What's more, she purchased four tickets for the dog show this weekend. She wasn't planning on leaving town, that's for sure."

"So where does that leave us?" Cherry cried.

"That leaves us with another mystery on our hands and no time to waste. Let's go to Gertrude Aimless's house and investigate," Jackie proposed.

Cherry brushed crumbs from the front of her shirt. She threw the food containers in the wastebasket and pocketed the fortune cookies for a late-night snack.

"Is she always this neat?" Jackie leaned over to Midge.

"She made me clean the car every hundred miles," Midge joked.

Cherry made a face at them both. "'It's always nice to come home to a tidy house,'" she said, quoting her mother. "Besides, you'll thank me for this later."

"*If* we come home," Midge mumbled.

They got into Jackie's car. She explained that it was an unmarked police car which she had borrowed from the station.

"Only they don't know it yet," she grinned. She drove expertly over the steep hills and through the heavy traffic. "Goodness, where is everyone going at this hour?" Cherry wondered aloud, checking her watch. "Why, it's almost nine p.m. If I'm not working, by this time on a Friday night I'm home in bed."

"Everyone here stays out all night dancing on Fridays," Jackie explained.

"Oh, my!" Cherry exclaimed. "I'd never be able to socialize all night. Why, I'd end up in bed all the next day."

"We'll see about that," Midge said. "As soon as we find Velma and your aunt, we're going to paint this town red."

Cherry secretly doubted that her Aunt Gertrude would ever go to a bar, but didn't want to dampen Midge's enthusiasm.

Why, if they could get out of this mess, Cherry would be willing to go anywhere Midge wanted!

CHAPTER 14

Missing!

It was obvious Aunt Gertrude hadn't been home for a while. A week-old newspaper was propped up in front of a cold cup of moldy coffee.

"She must have left in a pretty big hurry," Jackie said, pointing to two stale pieces of toast still in the toaster.

"Or had Aunt Gert been forced to leave?" Cherry wondered anxiously, looking around her aunt's tidy kitchen.

"Don't touch anything," Jackie cautioned as they looked around. A knock at the door startled them all.

"Get behind the door," Jackie said to Midge and Cherry as she took her revolver from its holster and peeked through the café curtains. Cherry thrilled at the sight of the girl in uniform boldly taking charge.

"It's just a kid," Jackie said. She opened the door and poked her head out. Cherry peeked and saw a slender lad clad in baggy overalls and a plaid shirt with a newsbag slung over his shoulder.

The boy's eyes widened at the sight of the police officer. "What's wrong, officer?" he asked. "Where's Gert?"

"I'm a friend of Gert's," Jackie said casually, determined not to alarm the child. "I'm watching the house for a while."

The boy said nothing and just stood there, shifting his weight from foot to foot.

"Is there anything you need?" Jackie asked.

"Yeah. Gert owes me for a month of papers."

"Isn't it a little late at night to be collecting?" Jackie wanted to know, as she dug in her pocket for some money. She paid the boy, but he still stood there. "Is there anything else?" she asked, puzzled by his queer behavior.

"Cookies," the boy said. "Gert always gives me some cookies to take home. I got a brother," he added. "But I don't give him any."

"That's nice," said Jackie, hoping he would just leave. "Gert's gone and I don't have any cookies for you, so you'll just have to leave. Good night." She shut the door, but she could see through the sheer curtains that the boy was still standing on the porch.

Jackie opened the door. "Honey, I don't have any cookies," she said gently.

"She keeps 'em in the cupboard next to the stove," he replied, walking right past Jackie into the kitchen. He opened a cabinet and pulled out a tin of chocolate chip cookies, stuffing one into his mouth.

"Where's Gert? She at church?" he asked, crumbs spilling down his chin.

"But Aunt Gertrude doesn't go to church!" Cherry cried, jumping out from behind the door. Cherry was puzzled by his remark. Her aunt was many things, but she was not religious!

"Grfh thy ashd asyu hj?" the lad replied.

"What?" the three girls asked in unison.

He swallowed his mouthful of cookie and brushed the crumbs from his face. "I said, what the heck's going on here? Why were you hiding? What kind of game is this?"

He eyed Cherry with interest. "Say, you're Gert's niece, right? Berry or Peach or something."

"My name's Cherry." She could feel a flush rising up her neck. "And who are you?"

"The name's Lauren," the lad replied. "Gee, you look just like Gert when she was in the army," he added.

Cherry looked puzzled. "My aunt was in the army? Really?"

The boy nodded. "Don't you know anything?" he scoffed. He went to the refrigerator and took out a bottle of milk. Before Cherry could stop him, he drank right from the bottle.

Cherry was annoyed. It was not only rude to drink right from the container, it was downright unsanitary. "Young man," she said, taking the bottle from him. "Where are your manners? Do you act like this at home?" she asked. She shuddered to imagine the kind of home this juvenile delinquent came from!

He burped and wiped his mouth on his sleeve. "Gert lets me drink it straight," he said in his defense.

"No matter," Cherry said briskly. "Now what's this church thing? What church?"

"I just meant that maybe she went somewhere with her nun friends. She usually spends the weekends with them." The boy looked worried. "Golly, is something wrong? Where's Gert? It's awful funny that she would leave the same weekend as the dog show."

Jackie didn't want to involve the teen, but she needed more information. "Can you keep a secret?" she asked.

"Sure. I keep tons of 'em. Got some myself," he bragged.

Jackie looked at Midge and Cherry, who nodded their approval. Jackie told Lauren about Gert's sudden departure, being careful not to mention the possibility of kidnapping. She cautioned him not to tell anyone.

"Gee, I wouldn't do anything to hurt Gert," he said, his eyes filling with tears. It was clear Gert meant a lot to the young man. Cherry regretted that she had been so harsh earlier and gave the lad a consoling hug. To her great surprise, under that baggy shirt were the soft curves of a young girl!

"Why, you're a girl!" she gasped.

Lauren blew her nose on her sleeve. "Sure I'm a girl. She took off her cap to reveal a long braid of sandy-colored hair. "I'm almost sixteen!"

"A girl," Midge said, with a laugh. "Well, I'll be."

The girl mistook her amusement for doubt. "You want me to take off my shirt?" she asked, starting to unbutton it.

Midge raised her eyebrows. "Keep your shirt on, girl."

Jackie broke in. "That's enough, girls."

"No matter what you are, you have atrocious manners!" Cherry scolded mildly.

Midge pinched Cherry on the arm to shut her up. "Don't be so charming, Cherry. We'll spank her later. Right now we need her help."

Midge was right. They needed all the help they could get, especially from someone who was familiar with Aunt Gert's habits. They resumed their search of the house, aided by Lauren, who had obviously spent many hours there. As the girl grew friendlier, Cherry warmed to her. They searched Gert's bedroom, and Cherry was pleased to find a photo of herself in her nurse's uniform, nicely framed and perched atop her aunt's bed table.

Cherry told Lauren how many times she had begged her parents to let her visit her favorite aunt. But they'd always said no. "Gert said I could come see her anytime and stay as long as I'd like," she remembered fondly.

"She talks about you all the time," Lauren said. "About how you're a nurse, and so smart and all."

They were interrupted by a muffled shout. Midge seemed to be calling from the next room, but when they ran into a small sitting room with plush chairs and oak bookshelves, Midge was nowhere to be seen!

This is crazy, thought Cherry, stopping to think for a moment. This reminded her of something that had happened to Nancy Clue in *The Case of The Sensible Shoes*. A ghostly voice had turned out to be that of a ventriloquist hiding in a nearby closet.

Cherry flung open the closet door, but, except for piles of neatly folded sweaters, it was empty. She wondered for a moment if Midge was playing a prank on them, but she immediately dismissed that idea. As fun-loving as Midge was, she knew when to be serious.

Cherry followed the muffled voice, which seemed to float out of the room and into the hallway. Suddenly, there was a knock on the wall right next to Cherry's ear. This time she really was frightened. "Suppose the house is haunted," she thought, "and there's a ghostly reason for Aunt Gert's disappearance?"

Cherry knocked on the wall, and the ghost knocked back.

"Why, it's a code," thought Cherry.

The ghost knocked twice. Cherry knocked twice.

Three knocks followed. Ditto, Cherry.

"If it would just continue, I'm sure I could crack the code," Cherry exclaimed, her ear to the wall. A few minutes went by, but there were no more knocks. She felt a draft from behind. Shivers ran down her spine. She whirled around to find Midge standing there with a big grin on her face.

"Shhh," said Cherry. "There's a ghost in the wall; it's trying to tell me something."

"Oh," Midge grinned. "Does it go like this?" She rapped three times on the wall.

Cherry looked puzzled. "How..."

"I'm the ghost," Midge laughed. "This way," she said to Cherry, leading her to the sitting room. Midge picked a book from the shelf and the massive oak bookcase swung silently open.

"Look—it's a secret passageway!" Cherry gasped.

"Good work," said Jackie, appearing behind them. "How did you think of looking for a hiding place?"

"I read it in a book when I was a kid. Remember Kit Karr, the girl detective? Once she was trapped in an evil professor's windowless study, and she escaped by finding the secret passageway in a bookshelf," Midge explained.

"I remember those books," Cherry cried. "My favorite was *The Kandy Kane Kaper*," she recalled, remembering the delicious delight of reading late at night under the covers, with only her flashlight for illumination.

Jackie interrupted their fond reminiscing. "We'll hold the book club later, girls," she said, as she slipped into the passageway. Cherry and Midge followed her lead, stumbling over each other as they groped their way through the darkness. Once they were inside, the bookshelf swung shut behind them. "We'll be trapped!" Cherry exclaimed.

"Don't worry," Midge said. "I know where the button is that opens the bookcase from the inside."

"Ouch!" Cherry cried. "Midge, stop stepping on my feet. If you had let me keep my purse, we'd have a flashlight right now," Cherry moaned, explaining that she always kept one in her handbag in case of an emergency. "Midge wouldn't let me carry my purse with this outfit," she explained. "She said it wasn't the, what was that word you used, Midge? Begins with a b?"

"Butch," Midge said. "It's not the butch thing to do." She pulled a book of matches from her pocket and handed them to Cherry. "Try these," she said.

Soon they came to a space large enough for two cots and a small chair. "Why, someone's been living here," Jackie said. Indeed, the small space bore evidence of human habitation. A teacup sat on the arm of the overstuffed chair, and the cots were heaped with warm blankets, including a quilt Cherry recognized as her aunt's handiwork.

On the floor next to one cot was a stack of books. "Look— Kit Karr mysteries!" Cherry cried, picking up *The Kase of The Kreepy Kave*. A piece of paper fell from between the pages of the book. "It's a map!" Cherry cried. "Perhaps it's a clue of some sort."

She held a match in front of the worn piece of paper. "It's

too dark in here to make it out. We'll look at it later, under better light," she declared. She put the paper in her pocket. They looked around for more clues.

"A child's been living here," Jackie said, picking up a worn stuffed bear from the cot. "This bear's been around for a long time," she said, noting the repaired stuffed arm and mismatched glass eyes.

"Why, it's Billy," Cherry said, gingerly taking the stuffed animal and holding it close to her bosom. "I gave this bear to Aunt Gert years and years ago, when my father kicked her out of the house. I snuck it in her suitcase at the very last minute." She tucked the bear under her arm. "We've simply got to find the child who was last with Billy," she declared.

A quick survey of the tiny room failed to turn up any more clues. As they headed back to the entryway, the last match fluttered, and then went out. And try as they might, they couldn't find the secret button that opened the passageway. "That darn escape button was right here a minute ago," Midge scowled.

"We're trapped!" Cherry cried.

"Be calm," Jackie said in a soothing voice.

"But I can't breathe," Cherry said, clutching her throat. She was beginning to feel dizzy.

"Don't be silly, Cherry," Midge teased. "People have been living here—there's obviously plenty of air."

Cherry blushed and realized that Midge was right. She was thankful that the darkness hid her embarrassment.

"Where's that kid?" Midge wanted to know. She started banging on the wall for Lauren. They could hear her muffled voice coming from the other side of the wall.

"Lauren, let us out," they called.

"Grh mun thk?" Lauren mumbled.

"Darn it, Lauren, swallow the darn cookie and listen!" Midge was really annoyed this time.

The girl did as she was told. "How do I get you out?" she called.

"It's a book on the third...no, fourth shelf. In the middle. Just take it off the shelf," Midge replied.

"What's it about?" Lauren wanted to know.

—— CHAPTER 15 ——

A Special Kiss

"It's up to you, Cherry. You've just *got* to find Nancy Clue," Jackie said as they dropped Cherry at the boarding house. Jackie's urgent words echoed in Cherry's ears as she climbed the three flights of stairs to her room. She shuddered as she thought of the places she would be investigating that evening—and all by herself! For they were sending her to taverns and dance clubs to find the wayward detective.

As much as she hated the idea of going to these places, she was glad that at the last minute she had decided to pack her best party frock: a stunning azure silk sheath with a matching chiffon overskirt that had seen little wear in the last year. Its simple styling was timeless, and at least Cherry didn't have to worry about looking like, well, like someone from Idaho!

She looked glumly at her current outfit. "I just wouldn't feel comfortable going out in this," she thought. She was, however, beginning to understand the allure of wearing men's trousers. She especially liked the deep, roomy pockets.

She wished the others could have come in for a moment and helped her get ready, but time was of the essence, and the sooner they reached the convent the sooner they could solve the ever-growing puzzle.

She quickly washed the sticky pomade out of her hair, and fluffed her short locks until they lay in a short wavy cap over her head.

"It will be nice to wear lipstick again," she thought. She remembered that girls in San Francisco looked more high-fashion than girls in Pleasantville, so she applied her cosmetics with a liberal hand.

Before donning her evening outfit, she folded her slacks and put them over the back of a chair. In the pocket she found the map from Aunt Gert's secret room!

"I'll tell you later," cried an exasperated Midge. "I am *never* having children," she added under her breath.

They could hear the girl rummaging all willy-nilly through the shelves. A moment later the door swung open. Lauren smirked at the trapped trio, her arms folded over her baggy overalls. "Aren't you going to thank me?" she wanted to know.

Midge just glowered at the girl.

Cherry tried to smooth things over and offered to help Lauren put the books back. "And neatly," she added, remembering that her aunt was particular about her precious books.

"Time for a private conference, girls," Jackie said, motioning Midge and Cherry into the bedroom next door. Lauren protested at being left behind, but, as Cherry was quick to point out, she hadn't finished putting back all the books.

They left a grumbling Lauren to her task and went into the bedroom. Jackie settled in a comfortable mossy green chintz chair, pulled out her notepad and started to write.

"What's up, officer?" Midge asked.

Jackie shook her head. "Nothing adds up," she said. "I hate to admit it, but I'm stumped! Somehow all these disappearances are connected, but I fail to see how. Cherry, Midge, is there something you haven't told me?"

Cherry flung herself on Aunt Gert's chenille-covered bed. "I don't know what else to tell you; all I know is that because of me, first Velma was kidnapped, and now Aunt Gert's disappeared." She started to cry. "I'm not only a terrible detective, I'm a danger to my friends!"

Midge found a handkerchief in the top drawer of the mahogany dressing table and handed it to the bereft nurse. Cherry dried her eyes. She noticed the monogram "C.M." on one corner of the lace-edged hankie. "Why, these aren't Aunt Gert's initials," she thought. "Where have I seen this before?"

Midge sat on the bed next to Cherry, looking pensive. "Maybe I should tell you..." But before she could continue, she was interrupted by a shout from Lauren.

"Hey, you guys, guess what?" Lauren called to them from the study.

"Not now," Jackie called back. "Midge, what were you going to say?"

But before Midge could answer, Lauren appeared at the

doorway holding a book of female nudes. Cherry grabbed the book away from the young girl.

Lauren snatched the book back. "Now just wait a gosh-darn minute," she scowled. "I've got to show you something."

Cherry covered her eyes. "I just won't look," she told herself, but when Jackie exclaimed, "Golly!" she just couldn't help herself. She opened her eyes, and when she saw what was in Lauren's hands, she, too, gave a little shriek.

"It's a photograph of my aunt and another woman dressed as nuns! But we're not even Catholic," she shrieked.

"Not just any nuns, Cherry," Jackie said excitedly. "The woman she's with is the Mother Superior of the order of nuns that's been snatched."

"And look at the car behind them!" Midge said excitedly. "Why, it's a convertible just like the car I saw Velma in earlier," Midge cried.

Jackie checked her notebook. "That must be Gertrude Aimless's car. This proves beyond a shadow of a doubt that Velma and Gertrude's disappearances are linked to the missing nuns case, but how?"

She frowned. "The bad news is there have been no clues in the case of the missing nuns. Why, the detectives downtown are so puzzled, they've issued a public call through the newspapers for Nancy Clue."

"I guess it's time we ask for the famous girl detective's help, too," Midge admitted grudgingly. "But where is she?" Midge looked at Cherry. "You seem to know a lot about this Clue girl. Where do you think she's gone?"

"The newspaper said she's staying with relatives. I'd just check the phone book under Clue," Cherry replied brightly.

Jackie shook her head. "We already tried that. I don't think Nancy really has anybody out here. I think she's all alone, and probably feeling pretty down about her father's murder." She paused dramatically. "There was a rumor going around the Black Cat last night that Nancy Clue had been in there earlier, hitting the bottle pretty hard," Jackie said. "I told the boys downtown that she had been spotted there, but they just laughed. I was planning on following that lead tonight."

"That's it!" Midge cried. "Gather round, gals. I've got a plan!" Jackie, Cherry and Lauren gave their full attention to Midge as she laid out her scheme.

"I propose we go to the convent and investigate on our own," she said.

"Yippee!" cried Lauren. "Let's go!"

"Hush, I'm not finished. Besides, we're not taking you with us," Midge said firmly.

But Jackie disagreed. "Lauren knows more about Gert than any of us," she argued.

"I think she's proven herself an invaluable help," Cherry pitched in.

Midge scowled. "You can go only if you promise to obey all orders," she said gruffly.

"Yes, ma'am," Lauren grinned, giving Midge the traditional three-fingered Girl Scout salute.

"And it's just that kind of smart-alecky attitude that's going to get us all in trouble," Midge snapped.

The air was tense. Cherry thought quickly. What could she do to smooth tensions between these two? "I'll be personally responsible for her," Cherry suggested brightly.

Midge shook her head. "Cherry, you've got to stay in San Francisco and look for Nancy Clue."

"Me?" cried Cherry. "I'll never be able to find her," she protested. "You've seen what a terrible detective I really am. Why, I wouldn't know where to begin. Why not send Lauren? She's forthright."

"If anyone can find her, you can, Cherry," Midge said. "You told me yourself you solved a mystery at your hospital." She turned to Jackie. "All the way here, it was Nancy Clue this and Nancy Clue that. Cherry knows more about her than anyone."

"We have faith in you, Cherry," Jackie said, putting her arm around Cherry's shoulders. "Someone's got to stay here and look for Nancy Clue. And if the rumor about her is true, this is no job for a kid!"

"Oh, no," she groaned. "I forgot all about this!" She slipped the map into her evening bag. "It's too late now," she thought. "Perhaps this will come in handy later."

She had just slipped into her dress when there was a knock at the door. "Yoo-hoo, it's Sally." Cherry reluctantly opened the door.

"May I borrow a cup of sugar?" Sally wanted to know.

"But there's no cooking allowed in the rooms," Cherry said, remembering the big sign behind the manager's desk. Sally just laughed and breezed past Cherry. She planted herself in the room's only chair. "Ha, ha. Only kidding. Call me silly Sally." She settled into the chair for what threatened to be a long chat, and lit a cigarette.

Cherry anxiously looked around for a no-smoking sign, but didn't see one. How could she possibly get rid of this girl? Normally she would have welcomed some company, even Sally's goofy chatter, but she had a mission to accomplish, and she could not be distracted.

"I'm very sorry, but I must be running along. I have an appointment," she said primly, putting her small silk clutch purse containing a lipstick, compact and clean handkerchief into the inside pocket of her dressy coat. Wrist-length gloves with cunning pearl buttons completed her outfit.

"The right accessories can make a good-looking dress into a really smart outfit," her mother always said.

"Your skirt's ripped!" Sally exclaimed. Cherry inspected the overskirt of her outfit. Sally was right! There was an ugly rend in the fabric.

"I don't have time to fix this!" she wailed. "Whatever will I wear?"

At Sally's suggestion, Cherry removed the torn overskirt of her frock, which simply unsnapped.

"I can't wear this dress without something over it," she said, looking at herself in the full-length mirror. "Why, without the overskirt, it's practically revealing!" Indeed, the snug line of the straight dress emphasized Cherry's curvaceous figure more than she cared for. "Maybe I can just keep my coat on," she thought, realizing none of her other outfits would do for that evening's assignment.

"Where are you going?" Sally asked.

"Er, ah, I'm meeting friends for a drink. And I'm already

late," Cherry stammered, her face all a-flush. She had never been a very good liar.

"Well, I'll be running along then," said Sally, moving toward the door. "Maybe I'll see you later. I usually hang out at The Black Cat on Friday nights."

Cherry recognized that name, for it was on the list Jackie had made for her, which was now stowed securely in her purse. "Perhaps I'll see you later," she said, locking the door behind her and heading downstairs.

As luck would have it, she found a taxi right away, and within ten minutes had arrived at the first place on her list. "This is one evening I'm not looking forward to," she murmured, taking a deep breath before entering the rough-and-tumble cowboy hangout. It was hard to see in the dim, smoky light. Cherry subtly checked out the crowded bar, looking for Nancy Clue's trademark mane of silky titian-colored hair. She walked around the perimeter of the dance floor, eyeing each corner of the room, but Nancy was nowhere to be seen.

Lively dance lessons were being given, and Cherry soon found herself tapping her feet to the music. The place was crowded with many couples, and as Cherry's eyes grew accustomed to the smoke, she realized that there were no men in the bar. She had never seen girls dancing together before.

"A perfect fit," Cherry murmured as she slipped off her coat.

A stocky brown-haired girl dressed in jeans and cowboy boots offered to show her some dance steps, and before Cherry could say anything, the girl whisked her off her stool and onto the dance floor. At first Cherry felt foolish, as the steps were new to her, but soon she caught on, and twenty minutes passed before she sat down again.

She and the girl relaxed over a tall pitcher of beer. Cherry kept meaning to leave, but she found the golden-skinned girl's lively chatter riveting. Cherry had never heard an accent like hers before. It sent shivers up and down her spine.

She reluctantly left the bar to continue her search, but not before getting the girl's phone number. She was sure that when the mystery was solved and everyone was safe, her chums would enjoy meeting this girl and hearing her fascinating tale.

"Perhaps we could all have a picnic supper together on the beach."

Her thoughts turned to her friends, who were racing toward the convent. She said a little prayer for them and hopped in a cab. The bar Sally had mentioned was next on her list.

Her dressy outfit was a little more appropriate here. Many of the other girls wore off-the-shoulder dresses and high heels. She was glad she had worn this dress after all, which she knew accentuated her light eyes and flattered her figure.

"Buy you a drink?" Cherry looked up into the face of a tall redhead with a Midwestern accent. The girl sat down and introduced herself as Chris. Cherry didn't want to be rude, but at the same time she did not want to encourage the attentions of this girl. She really must look for Nancy Clue! She was searching her mind for something to say when the girl jumped up.

"There's my girlfriend. Gotta go," she whispered hurriedly.

A cute woman with bleached-blond hair and a perky manner hopped onto the now-vacant stool. "Buy you a drink?" she asked in a cheerful, slightly raspy voice. This time Cherry nodded. After all, she *was* getting a little thirsty.

The bartender brought them each a frothy drink called a Pink Squirrel. The blonde playfully tucked the small paper umbrella that came with the drink behind one ear, wrinkled her small freckled nose and giggled. Her laugh was contagious, and soon Cherry was giggling, too.

She looked familiar, but Cherry couldn't place her.

"You look familiar," she said, immediately wishing she had said something more original. The woman just grinned and smoothed the legs of her tight-fitting white leather pants outfit. She adjusted her pink chiffon scarf, tied with a gay knot at her throat. She ran a hand through her short hair and grinned, showing off straight white teeth.

"Why, you're in the movies. You're my mother's favorite movie star!" gasped Cherry, finally recognizing the singing movie actress. "I just loved your latest movie. I saw it three times," she gushed, searching in her purse for a scrap of paper for an autograph. As usual, she had nothing to write on.

The actress took the umbrella from her hair and signed it.

"Golly, I'm all flustered. Wait until I tell Mother," Cherry gushed.

"Let's keep it our little secret, shall we?" the woman suggested slyly, ordering another round for the twosome.

Cherry agreed, a little disappointed that she couldn't share this moment with anyone. Yet she was thrilled at having met an honest-to-goodness movie star.

"What's Rock really like?" she asked, knowing her brother Charley would want to know about his favorite star.

The actress laughed. "He's at the Stud; you could catch him there." Cherry checked, but there was no bar by that name on her list.

They sipped their drinks. The actress got a little fresh—or was her hand on Cherry's thigh merely an accident? Cherry

politely excused herself, and the woman got the hint. She didn't seem at all offended, which relieved Cherry, who hated to hurt anyone's feelings.

"*Que sera sera*," the woman cried gaily as she hopped off her stool.

Cherry didn't know what she meant. "Oh, why didn't I pay more attention in high school Spanish class?" she berated herself. She resolved to resume her language studies as soon as she returned home. Determined not to get into any more uncomfortable situations, Cherry decided to visit the ladies lounge and refresh her lipstick. On the way she bumped into Sally.

"Hello, girl," Sally exclaimed, planting a big wet kiss on Cherry's cheek. Cherry was relieved to see someone she knew, even if it was silly Sally.

"So where's your great big good-looking friend in uniform?" Sally wanted to know, looking over Cherry's shoulder. "I was sure she'd be here. After all, it *is* Butch Night."

Cherry explained that Jackie and Midge had left town on business. Sally looked disappointed.

"I was here with Chris, but I lost her in the crowd, and now I see that her girlfriend's here, so I guess I'm single Sally now." Cherry's head swam. Nothing Sally said made any sense. But Cherry was tired of sitting in bars alone, feeling lost. She told Sally she was searching for her long-lost cousin, and invited her to come along. Sally liked the idea.

"But I've really got to be serious," Cherry warned.

"That's me—serious Sally."

They headed for a bar a few blocks away. The night air was chilly, and Cherry pulled her coat closer. Sally chattered all the way to the What If Club. They paid their dollar at the door and took seats at the bar.

The bartender served them tall frothy drinks topped with big chunks of fruit skewered on plastic swords. Cherry was reluctant to imbibe further—after all, she'd already had four drinks. "I'll just eat the fruit," she told herself and popped a cherry into her mouth. "Oh, just one tiny sip," she thought, tasting the sweet drink.

"This is delicious," she exclaimed to Sally, already on her second.

Sally introduced Cherry to the bartender, a friendly southern girl named Babe. "Good, huh?" asked Babe, pointing to the drink.

"It's the house special. It's called Tutti-Fruity."

"It's wonderful," giggled Cherry, feeling a little flushed. She emptied her glass. For the first time that evening, she was beginning to relax. Babe placed another drink in front of her, and before she knew it, that too was gone.

"Oh, dear," she thought. "I'd better slow down."

She turned to Sally to suggest they leave and find some food, which, as a nurse, Cherry knew would absorb some of the alcohol in her system. But Sally was gone!

Babe caught her puzzled expression. "You never know

when that girl's going to disappear," she confided. "Trust me; I should know."

Cherry was pondering Babe's cryptic comment when she felt someone at her elbow. An attractive girl with silky titian hair, startling blue eyes and a forward manner wanted to know if she was alone. Was she alone? Sally was nowhere to be seen.

The girl hopped onto the stool next to Cherry and ordered a sloe gin fizz. "And give my chum here another drink," she said, gesturing toward Cherry's empty glass.

Cherry knew she should be getting on with her search, but something about the titian-haired girl was so riveting she found herself unable to move on. She slyly checked her lipstick in her compact mirror. Suddenly, she desperately wanted to look her best!

The girl laughed. "You look lovely," she purred. She reached over and touched Cherry's hand ever so lightly. "You have such tiny hands," she said. "Like a child's." She toyed with the gold charm bracelet around Cherry's slim wrist. "How cute!" she cried. "You have a tiny nurse's cap on your bracelet."

"My mother gave it to me when I graduated from nursing school two years ago," Cherry said, a little flushed from the attention.

"That's nice," the girl said softly, a misty look in her eyes. "Tell me about yourself," she said. Afraid to divulge any information about the mystery she was working on, Cherry instead told the girl about life in Pleasantville, about her parents and her twin Charley, their summers together on their grandmother's farm, and about the day she found a bird with a broken wing and nursed it back to health, thus beginning her lifelong desire to be a nurse.

Cherry stopped talking, embarrassed by how much she had revealed.

"Go on," the girl urged. "It sounds like you had a wonderful childhood."

"It was just your average childhood," Cherry said. "What about your family?"

The girl shook her head. "I'm all alone in the world." She stared into space for a minute. "But let's not talk about me. I want to hear more about you."

"I have tons of hilarious nurse stories!" Cherry exclaimed.
The girl ordered more drinks. "Tell me all of them," she urged.
So Cherry did, and after a while, the girls felt like old
friends. Why, this girl was so easy to talk to, Cherry felt as if
she had known her forever!

Cherry's head felt fuzzy. She knew it was probably partly
the alcohol, but she felt a peculiar exhilaration being around
this girl.

"I know there's something I'm supposed to be doing," she
thought. "But for the life of me, I can't remember what it is!"

When the girl suggested they get some air, Cherry eagerly
agreed. She felt wonderful—all warm and tingly inside—but
there was something nagging at the back of her mind.

"Maybe some fresh air will wake me up," she thought,
checking her lipstick in the mirror behind the bar before slipping her coat over her shoulders.

She followed the titian-haired girl through a back door
that led to an alley. The girl lit a cigarette and leaned against
the brick wall. "Mind if I smoke?" she asked. Cherry shook
her head. If truth be known, she was too relaxed to mind anything right now!

The night air cut right through her silk dress. She pulled
her wrap closer.

"Don't do that," her companion whispered. "I like looking
at you."

The girl surveyed Cherry, looking her up and down. She
whistled, a long, low appreciative whistle.

Cherry dropped her coat.

"It's a full moon," the girl said. "You never know what will
happen."

A shiver went down Cherry's back, for she was having that
very same thought.

Cherry began to wish she had worn panties. She had decided against them so as to preserve the line of her dress, but
they would be a big help right now.

The air was so still and quiet, she was sure the girl could
hear her heart beating. She was wondering what to do next,
when the decision was made for her.

The girl finished her cigarette. She leaned over and kissed
Cherry, first on her neck and then full on her mouth. She ca-
ressed her breasts through the silk dress.

"This shouldn't be happening," Cherry thought. "Why, I don't even know her name." But it didn't matter. She kissed the girl back with all her might.

It took the headlights of an approaching patrol car to pry the two girls apart. Cherry pulled down her dress, which had somehow become hiked up over her thighs. They ran into the street and quickly found a cab. Cherry didn't know where she was going, and, frankly, she didn't care!

Within minutes they were at the girl's motel suite. The sitting room was strewn with clothing, jewelry and half-empty containers of take-out food. The girl switched on the hi-fi.

"Sinatra okay?" she asked. Cherry nodded.

The girl dropped her velvet evening jacket on the floor and swayed into the tiny kitchenette.

She returned a few minutes later with two snifters of brandy, and waved Cherry in the direction of the davenport. The girl settled into an easy chair and sipped her drink.

Cherry suddenly felt embarrassed. What should she do next? What would Midge do, she wondered?

She blushed. She knew just what Midge would do in this situation!

The girl stretched and yawned, looking very much like a sleek and soft cat. Cherry had a vision of the girl purring, and she tingled at the thought. She took a sip of brandy. As the warm liquid slid down her throat, she began to relax, and before she knew it, she was stretched out on the couch with her shoes off, telling more stories about her life as a big city nurse.

"I used to be like you," the girl said sadly. "I had work I cared about. But now I just can't seem to focus on anything." The girl didn't seem to want to say more, so Cherry didn't press her.

The girl looked into her glass, as if looking for an answer. "I know where I could get work," she said, "but I'm not sure I'm up to it."

Cherry meant to ask her what she did for a living; she meant to ask her a lot of things. But, somehow, something else came up.

CHAPTER 16

An Unexpected Awakening

"Where am I?" gasped Cherry, trying to focus her blurry eyes. "Golly, it's bright in here!" she groaned, burying her face in her pillow. Suddenly she bolted out of bed. "Oh, no!" she cried, clutching her head. "Now I remember what I was supposed to be doing last night!"

She wasn't alone. The attractive titian-haired girl was asleep next to her, with only a thin sheet covering her naked body. "Golly," gulped Cherry as she realized she was naked, too. She ran to the small bathroom, practically tripping over a pile of stockings and lingerie on the floor. The sink was littered with cosmetics. She quickly splashed some cold water on her face. She noticed a girl's robe hanging on the back of the bathroom door with the monogram "N.C." on the pocket.

She racked her brain for her hostess's name. "Nadine? Norine? Nina? Why can't I remember anything?" she groaned, donning the robe so she could search for her clothing without catching a chill.

After a quick tour through the messy motel suite, she located her slip in the kitchenette, and her dress on the back of the couch. She blushed when she remembered how she had lost it the night before.

Her stockings were nowhere to be found, so she decided to throw caution to the wind and go out onto the street barelegged.

"You in a hurry?" A sleepy voice called from the doorway. The girl brushed her long silky hair from her forehead and wrapped the thin sheet tighter around her body. Even in the harsh morning light she looked lovely. "You want some coffee? Or some breakfast?" the girl blinked.

Cherry shook her head. "Good thing," the girl laughed.

"I'm a terrible cook, although I do make a pretty decent cup of instant coffee. We had a housekeeper the whole time I was growing up, and she waited on me hand and foot. Now look where I ended up," she said ruefully, waving her hand at the piles of clothing and newspaper strewn about the messy room. "In this depressing place, filled with sterile, serviceable furniture."

Cherry folded the borrowed robe and put it on the couch. She rummaged through her purse for some cab fare. "I really have to be going," she said.

The girl looked disappointed. "Are you in town long?" she asked.

"I don't know," Cherry said truthfully. "I'm with some people and our plans are uncertain. I'm really dreadfully sorry I have to go like this. Perhaps I could call you later?" Cherry realized she would like to spend more time getting to know this girl. A lot more time. She blushed.

"Gee, you're even cuter when you blush," the girl giggled. She scribbled her phone number on a torn piece of paper. "Well, then, suppose you call me sometime?"

Cherry put the slip of paper in her purse. As anxious as she was to stay, she was even more anxious to resume her search for Nancy Clue. On her way out the door, she realized she hadn't even told the girl her name.

"By the way, I'm Cherry Aimless, R. N., from Seattle."

The girl laughed, took her by the hand and pulled her close. She kissed her. "I'm Nancy. Nancy Nobody. From Nowhere!" She laughed at her own joke. Her blue eyes sparkled.

"I've seen those eyes before last night," Cherry thought. Suddenly it came to her. "Why, you're Nancy Clue!" Cherry exclaimed.

"Guilty," Nancy said, not looking at all pleased that her secret was out.

"I was looking for you last night," Cherry cried.

"Oh, golly," Nancy grimaced. "I hope you're not here to tell me you're my long-lost sister."

Cherry laughed so hard that she had to sit down. "I'll take that cup of coffee now," she said. "You'd better make it strong. Have I got a story to tell you!"

Nancy sat quietly as Cherry told her everything. The party girl from last night had been replaced by a solemn and clear-headed sleuth. She was suddenly Nancy Clue, girl detective, again.

"We can't call the police," Cherry said. "Midge won't say why, but she's adamant about not letting anyone we don't really know in on this. I think she's hiding something, and when this is all over, I intend to find out what. The officer who is helping us is doing it on the sly," she explained.

"I used to think the police were my friends," Nancy said. "But after the last few days..." Her voice trailed off.

Cherry took her hand. "I know all about the murder of your father," she said. "I read about it in the newspaper. That's how we knew you were in San Francisco staying with relatives."

"I don't have anybody here," Nancy said sadly. "When I got to town, I put on dark glasses and a scarf and checked into this motel. Hannah told me to forget about the past and start a new life." Nancy burst into tears.

"But I just can't," she sobbed, wiping her tears on the clean handkerchief Cherry had quickly fished out of her purse. Cherry waited for an explanation, but none followed. Nancy looked lost.

Suddenly she snapped out of it. "We'd better hurry," she said. "We've got a lot to do."

"First I've got to go back to my room and change!" Cherry cried. "I can't possibly chase anyone in this tight dress."

"There's no time to waste," Nancy said. "Your chums could be in terrible danger. We've got to get to the convent." She looked Cherry up and down. "I'd say we were about the same size. I'm sure I've got something that will fit you." Nancy went to the bedroom and brought back three pieces of powder-blue luggage embossed with her initials.

"I left in kind of a hurry, so I didn't get to pack much," she said, pulling blouses and skirts from the largest suitcase. "But I think we'll find something suitable. That silk sheath looks divine on you, Cherry, but for where we're going, these make more sense." She handed her a pleated skirt and simple blouse.

Cherry slipped into the outfit, and checked herself in the mirror. "These heels look silly with this outfit!" she cried, staring at Nancy's impossibly small feet. "But I guess I'm stuck with them."

"You look adorable," Nancy said, kissing her on the nape of her neck. She threw a red wool car coat over her own outfit, tossed Cherry a sweater and found her car keys. "Let's go!" she cried.

It was almost noon by the time they backed Nancy's sporty yellow convertible out of the garage and headed toward the convent. Nancy handled the swift car with skill, and for once Cherry paid no heed to traffic laws, urging Nancy to drive faster and faster.

"I didn't think I'd ever race to the scene of a mystery again," Nancy said happily as she expertly steered her car through city traffic. "And I never dreamt I'd be in such beautiful company."

Cherry smiled. All this would be so thrilling, she thought, if only she didn't have the most dreadful feeling that her chums were in terrible danger!

CHAPTER 17

Held Captive

Cherry would have broken any number of speeding laws racing to the convent had she known the dilemma her chums were already in!

By the time Cherry had hopped onto the bar stool at The Black Cat and was sipping her second Pink Squirrel with a certain blond movie star, her chums had already arrived at the outskirts of Napa Valley, eighty miles northeast of San Francisco. They were driving slowly through the moonlight, searching the vine-covered landscape for the road that would lead them to the convent.

The drive to Napa had been a breeze, except that Midge couldn't stop worrying about Cherry. "I feel bad about sending that shy kid out into the night all by herself," she confessed to Jackie, keeping her voice low so as not to awaken Lauren, who was sound asleep in the back seat.

"Well, if Cherry's not actually here, at least she's here in spirit," Midge added with a laugh, indicating the pile of carefully folded maps in a leatherette portfolio under the seat.

"I couldn't help but notice you got us here without having to check any of those maps," Jackie said.

"Oh, I was up here once a long time ago," Midge answered casually. "But it's changed a lot. Perhaps if we drive around a bit, I'll remember which road leads to the convent property."

"What in the world would have brought you, of all people, to a convent, of all places?" Jackie quizzed her.

"Once I thought I might take the veil," Midge said quickly.

"Will wonders never cease," Jackie laughed.

While they searched in the dark for the right road, Jackie told Midge everything she knew about The Sisters of Mercy.

Midge listened with a studied attentiveness. "It's a self-sufficient teaching order," Jackie said. "The nuns support their school for girls by growing grapes for local vineyards. Rumor has it that the church wants to take back the convent from the good sisters and develop the land into a retirement home for priests. The locals are sure to fight that. Everyone considers the nuns to be a calming influence in an unstable region. For as serene as this area seems, this county has the highest rate of runaway wives in the state!" she revealed. "It's the funniest thing. These women seem to vanish into thin air."

"Imagine that," Midge said, turning her face to the window.

"Imagine being married," Jackie shuddered. The girls had a good laugh.

Suddenly Jackie jammed on the brakes, narrowly missing a deer bounding across the road. Lauren jerked awake. "Are we there yet?" she groaned.

"We'll be there in a few minutes," Midge assured her. "Turn here," she said, pointing out a dirt road to the left. Soon Jackie was navigating dark, bumpy country roads with only the moon and the stars to guide her.

"If memory serves, we should be behind the convent soon," Midge said, peering into the darkness ahead.

Just then Jackie noticed a pair of headlights in the rear-view mirror.

"Gee, this must be a popular joint. Who else would be visiting a convent at this hour?" Jackie wondered.

The car that had been behind them sped past, almost side-swiping them. "That's Gertrude's car," Lauren shouted. The car turned onto a side road and stopped suddenly. Jackie turned off her headlights and pulled over. She peered at the scene through her binoculars.

A tall man wearing a long black overcoat got out, opened the trunk and took out state police roadblocks. He blocked the road and roared away.

"Those are fake roadblocks!" Jackie cried. "Look—he's added an extra "e" on the end of the word police!"

"Let's move them and follow him," Lauren urged excitedly.

"He's headed for the convent," Midge said. "I think we'd attract less attention if we followed him on foot. It's not that far."

Jackie got out of the car, opened the trunk and took out a tool box. Inside was an assortment of tools, rope and pipes of various lengths and weights.

"I got this from my locker at police headquarters," Jackie explained, "for those days when I need extra, added protection."

"From criminals?" Lauren asked.

Jackie laughed bitterly. "No, from my *fellow* cops!"

"Pipes make great weapons," Midge said with a grin.

"And they can't be traced," added Jackie.

"And they're easy to hide," said Lauren, picking up a pipe and sliding it down one leg of her overalls and into her boot. Midge and Jackie did the same, Jackie tucking her service revolver into her belt.

"Who's got the map Cherry found at Aunt Gert's?" Jackie asked.

"Don't you have it?" Midge asked.

Jackie shook her head. "I thought you had it."

Midge groaned. "I bet Cherry has it. Some detectives we are," she said. "We can't even hang on to the one clue we do manage to find!"

"Cherry did leave us the teddy bear," Lauren pointed out.

"Great," Midge grumbled. "Some help a stupid stuffed bear will be."

Lauren tucked the bear into the front pocket of her overalls. "He'll hear you," she admonished. Midge groaned.

"Let's go, girls," Jackie said. "This is no time for regrets. We'll do the best we can with what we've got."

Midge led the way. Although Jackie had a flashlight, they were afraid the strong beam would attract attention, and so they stumbled along in the darkness. They gingerly made their way through the thick brush surrounding the convent, aware that the dense foliage could be hiding anything.

"Or anyone," Midge shivered to herself. "Be careful," Midge whispered to her companions as they drew closer to the convent. "The building is ringed with old rose bushes, which have really big thorns. It's an allusion to Christ's crown of thorns," she explained. "It's a medieval practice."

They heard a twig snap somewhere ahead of them. The trio ducked behind the trunk of a thick old redwood. Jackie drew her revolver. "It sounds like someone's marching back and forth," she whispered.

"We're very close to the main portal of the convent," Midge said. "Someone must be guarding it."

Just then the full moon broke free of a cloud, and shone upon the spooky scene, providing the girls with enough light to clearly see their foe.

"There's someone in a flowing white robe guarding the entrance. And he's got a rifle," Jackie gasped.

Lauren took Jackie's binoculars and peered through them. "That's an altar boy," she said. "I know because when I was a kid, I wanted to be one, but Father Buchanan said girls weren't allowed that close to the Sacred Host."

"Look," Midge cried, grabbing the binoculars from Lauren and training them on the lower part of the large stone building. "There's something going on in the cellar," she whispered sharply, handing the binoculars back to Jackie.

"See? There's a thin beam of light showing through the basement window."

"This proves without a doubt that someone is hiding something in there," Jackie exclaimed. "But how would they have gotten them there? The police already went over these grounds with a fine-tooth comb, and found nothing. That's why we haven't seen any patrol cars in the area. They've already given up here," Jackie informed them.

"I say we jump the altar boy and get inside," Midge proposed. Lauren seconded the idea.

As soon as the altar boy turned his back, the girls raced towards him, with pipes in hand. He twirled around just in time to see them coming.

"Jesus Christ!" he yelled when he spied the girls.

Jackie pulled her gun on him. "Shut up!" she said in an angry whisper, grabbing his gun. "One peep out of you and there'll be one fewer altar boy at mass next Sunday!" she threatened.

"I'm not afraid of you," he sneered. "Why, Father will be here any minute with five armed deacons, and they'll take care of you girls."

"Wanna bet?" Midge replied. She grabbed the muscular lad by the collar and raised him high in the air.

"Please don't hurt me," he whimpered.

"Where's Velma?" Midge demanded.

"Who?" the boy asked, his voice quavering.

"You know. She was kidnapped and brought here. She's got dark hair, and was wearing a yellow dress."

"If you put down that gun, I'll tell you everything," the boy whimpered.

But instead of keeping his promise, he cried for help. Jackie grabbed him. "I ought to do you in right here," she said.

"Wait," Midge interrupted.

"Yeah, wait. You wouldn't dare harm an altar boy," he said arrogantly.

Midge slugged him, knocking him unconscious. "What I meant to say was, wait, a gun will make too much noise. That should keep the arrogant little brat quiet for a few hours."

"We'd better get moving," Jackie said. "He said his father was going to be here any minute."

"And look! The light from the cellar's been extinguished. We've got to hurry," Midge said. She jerked the robe off the limp boy and handed it to Lauren. "Here—put this on and pick up that rifle. Quick," she whispered. "I hear footsteps coming this way."

Lauren donned the billowy white robe and took her post, while Midge and Jackie ducked behind a rosebush and prayed that Lauren would pull off the charade.

"She's really quite good," Midge thought, noticing that Lauren gave a convincing performance as an arrogant altar boy. She even remembered to spit now and then. "Why, she's a born Girl Scout," Midge thought proudly.

The man they had seen drive up in Aunt Gert's car opened the thick wooden front door and poked his head out.

"Joe, is everything okay out here?" he asked.

Lauren grunted her reply. The man seemed satisfied, and went away.

"I recognize that man," Jackie whispered. "My god, it's Father Helms. His picture was in the newspaper along with the story about the church taking this land from the sisters. If the missing nuns are really trapped in there, that makes him the ringleader. Why, if that's true, this case is even bigger than anyone imagined!"

"I heard him talking to someone," Lauren reported as she joined them. She struggled out of the billowy robe. "Right as he closed the door, some guy said something about that stubborn nurse not giving them what they wanted. Then the other one said he had ways of making her talk!"

"I must get in there and save Velma!" Midge cried. "This is so frustrating! I have what they want, but they don't know it."

She pulled the book from her jacket pocket. "This contains something that priest wants desperately, but what is it? I've looked through it over and over, but I've found nothing." She fell to her knees. "Oh, Velma!" she sobbed. "Where are you?"

"Look," Jackie cried, pointing to the book, which had fallen open on the ground beside Midge. "Could this be something?" She picked up the well-worn novel. "See how the spine here is broken? Maybe this page contains a clue of some sort."

"'The heart of every convent is the chapel,'" she read. "And it's been underlined. It might be a clue."

"The chapel—I think I remember how to get there," Midge said, composing herself. "Stay low to the ground so no one can see us."

They made their way in the dark, clinging to the rough stone of the building. Soon they came to a series of low, wide windows.

"This is the refectory," Midge whispered. "It's where the nuns take their meals. Get down!" she hissed suddenly. "There's someone in there!"

"Look!" Lauren whispered. "Nuns!"

Lauren was right. Coming through the long narrow room were three nuns, each holding a tray of steaming food. And Father Helms was behind it all, with a gun trained on them! The group turned a corner and disappeared into darkness.

"That looks like a lot of food for one puny priest," Jackie commented. "They're either feeding the nuns, or..."

"Or there's more of his kind inside," Midge shivered. "Why, for all we know, there's legions of evil priests all over this place. And they could all be armed." She looked around. "Where's Lauren?" she cried, alarmed that the young girl seemed to have disappeared.

"Over here," Lauren called, taking care to keep her voice low. She was calling through the refectory window!

"Come in through that side door," she added, pointing to a small passageway near the kitchen. "And stop chatting so much. You'll give us away."

"She's a smug little twerp, but awfully handy," Midge grinned to herself as she made her way inside.

"Lauren, how did you find a way in? All the doors we've tried are locked."

"I used my matches to melt the leading on a stained glass window," Lauren bragged. "I managed to remove a piece big enough for me to slip through."

They tiptoed to the chapel, Midge reciting from the book as they walked. "'The centerpiece of any religious order is its chapel, especially if such chapel is lucky enough to contain a relic.'"

"What's a relic?" Jackie asked.

"We studied relics last week at Sunday School," Lauren reported. "It's a bone or a fragment from a saint with a shrine built around it. Sometimes they have a statue made that looks like the saint—only dead—and put the bone in that. Keen, huh?"

"That's very colorful," Jackie said. "I had no idea the Catholic Church had such tasteful traditions."

"I can tell you guys all kinds of really cool stuff," Lauren bubbled.

"We will certainly look forward to that," Midge said dryly. "Now hush up before they hear us!"

They had arrived at the chapel without incident. "The door to the sacristy is open," Lauren said. For Jackie's benefit, she explained that the sacristy was a special room where priests' vestments are kept.

"No one except priests are ever allowed in there," she said

solemnly. "Why, you could go straight to hell!"

"This is a bad time to worry about hell, Lauren," Midge said. "Let's go check it out." The sacristy was a small room paneled in the finest oak. Inside were many vestments sewn of the finest silks. "I think this is gold thread," Midge reported.

"I read somewhere that the nuns who sew these eventually go blind because of the little tiny stitches," Lauren said. "Wow, look at this chalice. It's pure gold."

"Oops!" Midge cried. "I knocked over these little white things." She picked up a box containing paper-thin wafers and popped one in her mouth. "Blah," she said. "Too dry."

"Jeepers! It's the body of Christ!" Lauren cried. "Spit it out!"

"Look over here," Jackie said, gesturing Midge and Lauren over to the large round table that dominated the room. She pointed to large sheets of paper containing sketches of a building. "These are the blueprints for that retirement center the church wants to build on this land!" she exclaimed.

The girls studied the sketches thoughtfully. "It looks like they're planning on razing this entire building. They're going to put a golf course right where the vineyards are!"

"And here's the swimming pool. Boy, this whole thing looks like one big playground, doesn't it?"

"Let's see what else they're planning," Jackie said, digging through the pile of papers on the table. "This is a will made out in the name of the Catherine MacCaffry." She skimmed the document. "This is her family land and, according to this will, all of it will go to the church upon her death."

"But it hasn't been signed," Midge pointed out.

"I bet that evil priest is holding the sisters hostage until she signs this!" Jackie exclaimed.

"*That's* why she ran away to Seattle," Midge murmured. "And somehow, she ended up in Cherry's hospital."

Jackie glared at her. "What do you mean, 'ran away to Seattle'? Who is she? What else are you hiding?" she demanded.

"Oops! Did I forget to mention that Cherry's amnesia patient Lana and the Mother Superior—I mean, this MacCaffry woman—are the same person?" Midge blushed. "You see, the way I figure it..."

A loud scream coming from the chapel interrupted them. Midge whirled around. "What's that darn Lauren up to?" she groaned. "If she doesn't clam up, she's going to give us away!" Midge and Jackie raced out of the sacristy. They found a wide-eyed Lauren with her hand clasped over her mouth. She looked like she had seen a ghost!

"Pipe down!" Midge hissed.

"But it's real!" Lauren gulped, pointing to a life-sized statue standing next to the altar.

"It's just a statue," Midge said, examining the bulky white stone figure. "You only thought it was a real body because it's dressed in real clothes. Catholics dress up their statues sometimes." She pointed to the gold plaque on the wall next to the figure. "See—it says, 'Saint Kellogg, Patron of the Harvest.'"

Although Midge tried to reassure Lauren, she had to admit to herself that the ghostly white figure, with its blank, staring eyes was pretty scary!

Lauren shook her head. "Its face...I touched it...Look!"

Midge grudgingly stepped closer to the figure. "Lauren, how on earth did you manage to poke a hole in this thing?" Midge touched the crumbling surface of the saint's face. "Why, this is just plaster! It breaks right off. *Ugh!* It's *squishy* underneath! Oh, my god, Lauren, you're right! It *is* real! A real dead man!" Midge jumped back.

Jackie took charge, conducting an expert analysis of the scene. "This is a deceased Caucasian adult male," she declared. "Someone's tried to hide the body by plastering it and wiring the resulting 'statue' to the wall...There's a large dent in the rear portion of his skull. I'd say he died from a blow from a blunt instrument."

She checked his hands. "There's dirt under his nails, which indicates he was probably killed and buried somewhere else, and then dug up and hidden here."

"You're all very bright girls," a sinister male voice rang out from the darkness. "It's just too bad I'm going to have to kill you."

CHAPTER 18

A Confession

"I can't believe we let those horrible men capture us!" Midge wailed, kicking the cold stone wall of their cell. "We should have just taken our chances and shot our way out," she added angrily.

"Right, Midge. My gun against five heavily-armed deacons," Jackie said. "We'd all be dead by now. Besides, what makes you think we're going to be trapped in here for long?"

"Oh, I don't know," Midge answered in a sarcastic manner. "Perhaps it's the thick iron door, padlocked behind us. That, and the fact that nobody knows we're here. You said yourself you didn't tell anyone where you were headed, remember?"

Midge began to pace the tiny cell, measuring no more than ten square feet. "I'm acting like a jerk," she admitted. "It's just that being locked up drives me crazy!"

She did the deep-breathing exercises Cherry had taught her during their car trip from Oregon, but they didn't work. "I don't need to relax, darn it, I need to escape!" she thought.

"Let's search for a way out," Lauren suggested. "Maybe we can find a secret passage."

"Don't you think I'd know about it?" Midge snapped. "I mean...uh...I don't know what I mean," she stammered. Midge slumped to the cold dirt floor. "I am not at my best right now," she apologized.

"How would you know if there were a secret passage here, Midge?" Jackie prodded. "You keep alluding to the fact that you've been here before, yet I have a funny feeling it wasn't for a religious retreat."

"And why does being locked up make you so crazy?" Lauren interjected. "Midge, I think there's something you're not telling us. Now, spill the beans!"

"Spoken like a true detective," Jackie said. "Well, Midge?"

"I really need a cigarette if I'm going to go into all this," Midge stalled.

Lauren produced a squished pack of cigarettes from her overalls pocket. "They're only a few months old," she said. "Here, you can keep 'em all."

Midge lit a cigarette and inhaled deeply. "Funny, I've been waiting to tell this story for years, but all of a sudden, I feel nervous," she confessed. "Okay, here goes. I haven't always been Midge Fontaine. My real name is Hallie Hoover!"

"Hallie Hoover! You mean the California teenager who was convicted of attempted patricide almost twenty years ago and sentenced to life in prison? The one who escaped from the federal pen after five years, and has been missing ever since?" Jackie cried.

"So I take it you've heard of me?" Midge said in a bemused manner.

"Girl, you were the talk of the West Coast for a long time. Why, every time I acted up, my mother would compare me to you, which secretly pleased me," Jackie grinned.

"You were in jail for five whole years?" Lauren cried. "Five years? Why, that's a whole third of my entire lifetime!"

"Thank you for that reminder," Midge said.

"Oh, gee, Midge, I didn't mean anything by it."

"I know, kid. I just have a hard time thinking about those days. Although, if I hadn't gone to prison, I would have never met Velma."

"Velma's a convict too?" Lauren cried delightedly. "This story is getting better by the moment."

Midge laughed, picturing the pretty Velma behind bars. "I met Velma in jail, but she wasn't behind bars," she said.

"But wait. Let me begin at the beginning." Midge stretched out on the cold stone floor, using her jacket as a pillow. "I think we'll have enough time," she said.

She lit another stale cigarette, and continued.

"Horrible Hallie, the newspapers called me. Said I was the kind of girl who gave teenagers a bad name. I lived in Santa Cruz. Actually, it was a lot like the town Cherry's from. A nice small town. Neat little houses with tidy front yards.

"Except our house wasn't so nice. My dad drank a lot, and when he did, he was horrible to us kids. One day I ran away from home. I took his savings; he kept it in a sock drawer in his bureau. I took his gun, too.

"I went to my best friend's house, a nice Catholic girl named Margaret O'Malley. I just went to say good-bye. I was going to hit the road, ride the rails. I could have just blended right in. My plan was to pass as a boy; I figured it would be safer that way.

"Peg told me about this really sweet nun she knew who really liked to help young girls. While we were talking, my dad showed up at her house and started beating the bejesus out of me.

"So, I shot him, and Peg and I ran. I found out later I didn't kill him, but I came pretty darn close.

"We went to see that nun, and she brought us here. Her aunt—the Mother Superior at that time—is retired now. But for years she was many girls' link with a better life.

"She helped me and Peg disappear. She got papers for us, new identification cards, even money. Peg had her make up a high school diploma, and letters of recommendation, and with it, she got a scholarship to a nursing school in Seattle, where she practices today, as Head Nurse Margaret Marstad.

"In fact, she's Cherry's boss at the hospital."

"Does Cherry know all this?" Jackie cried.

Midge shook her head. "Those of us who have gone through the underground agree to protect one another's identities," Midge said, adding, "I'm only telling you this because I'm sure we're never getting out of here.

"Anyway, I was so grateful to the nuns, I decided to work for them. Believe it or not, I wasn't arrested taking someone across state lines, or carrying forged I.D. papers, or any of the illegal things I used to do. I was picked up during a raid on a bar, and when they ran a check on me, they discovered the old warrant for my arrest for the attempted murder of my father.

"As if he hadn't nearly killed me every time he was drunk," she said bitterly.

"So I was sent to jail, where I met Velma. She was my English teacher. I fell instantly in love, and we began a torrid affair from afar. She helped me escape," Midge said proudly.

"No one ever suspected her. As Velma says, everyone just thinks of her as an old maid school teacher. That term sounds so dry. Not at all like Velma," Midge chuckled.

"And now it ends here. Funny, I'm back at the place where my freedom began. And except for a few hard times, it wasn't too bad a ride."

"We're going to get out of here," Jackie assured her. "And when we do, I'm going to destroy all the records on you, Midge. I have friends all over the state. When we're finished, there'll be no trace of you in any police file anywhere."

"Let's search for a way out!" Lauren cried.

"The moon's full, so we have some light," Midge said hopefully, joining the search. They ran their hands over the rough stone walls. "Isn't it odd that a convent would have prison cells?" Jackie commented.

"Well, this is a cell, but it's not for prisoners. Twenty years ago, these were the nuns' bedrooms," she said. "In fact, I spent my first night in this convent in a room just like this."

"Gosh, you've lived so long and had so many adventures," Lauren said breathlessly.

"Haven't you had any adventures yet?" Jackie teased.

"Just one. My best friend and I were fooling around but my mother walked in on us. I told her we were conducting an experiment for health class, but I don't think she believed me. She's watched me like a hawk ever since."

"So how come they left you alone when they went on vacation?"

"Oh, I have a babysitter. My gym teacher, Miss Rutherford. She's probably asleep, though. She's pretty old—at least thirty-five."

"Thirty-five!" Midge gasped. "And she's still teaching? At *that* age?"

"You're making fun of me!" Lauren cried, stamping her foot. As she did, a small stone fell out of the wall to reveal a tiny opening.

"Lauren, you doll!" Jackie cried. Midge shone the flashlight down the opening. The small opening was narrow—not big enough for a hand—yet seemingly endless.

Midge peered into it. "What could possibly fit through here?" she asked. Just as she did, something came running out at them!

The three girls jumped back as a small brown mouse flew out of the wall and landed at their feet.

"Just like home," said Midge, kneeling on the cold stone

floor. She put out her hand and the mouse jumped into her palm. It scurried up her arm to her shoulder, and nibbled on her ear.

"Oh, it's tame," Lauren said, petting the tiny, light brown mouse.

The mouse seemed to enjoy the attention. It jumped into Midge's hair and began to squeak. Midge pulled it from her hair and placed it in her palm, rubbing its stomach. "Look, it's wearing a thin silver chain around its neck!" she cried. "She's definitely trained. That gives me an idea. But first, I need a pen."

Lauren reached into her baggy overalls and pulled out an assortment of writing tools.

"Got any paper in there?" Midge asked.

Lauren shook out the entire contents of her pocket, but was unable to find even a scrap of paper.

"I hate to do this," Midge said, taking Lana's book from her pocket. "But it looks like this is the only paper we've got."

"Don't tell anyone," she said as she gently peeled back the end paper from the inside cover of the book. She found that the paper had been glued using a minimum of paste, and pulled up easily from the inside cover. "It comes right off," she said happily. "I can probably fix it later, and no one will ever know."

She worked the paper until she could tear off a two-inch square. On a scrap of the paper, Midge wrote:

IS THAT YOU, KITTY?

"My nickname for Velma," she explained with a sheepish grin.

Midge wrapped the note around the tiny neck and secured it with the chain. She petted the little animal and shooed it down the tiny tunnel. The mouse scampered away.

"She knows what to do," said Midge. "I know my rodents. I once spent a great deal of time training small animals to do amusing things."

It seemed for now their fate was in the hands of this tiny creature. They sat down to wait. Midge picked distractedly at the ripped book.

"What's this?" she exclaimed, finding a small envelope stuck between the end paper and the cover. She carefully pulled it out and opened it. "There's a negative in here!" she cried.

Even with the moonlight shining in on them, it was too dark to make out a photographic negative clearly. "Lauren, hand me your matches. You don't have a magnifying glass on you, do you?" Jackie joked.

"Cherry would have one," Midge noted.

Even with the match, it took a bit of examining to make out the image.

"There's a girl posing on a rock," Jackie said, describing what she was seeing. "She's naked. She's not bad looking, either," Jackie reported, in a matter-of-fact tone. "Behind her is a man. It's hard to see, but it looks like he's wearing a long black outfit."

Midge took a look. "Why, I think it's Father Helmes. And he's—what's this? He's dragging a body!"

"I bet it's that corpse we saw in the chapel!" Jackie exclaimed.

"This is great!" Lauren said. "All we have to do is convince him to trade Velma for this negative!"

"But that's not enough," Midge said. "We have to find a way to protect the convent. If they go through with their plans to turn it into a playground for priests, they'll destroy an important institution for females on the run."

"So many lives are at stake here," Jackie said somberly. "We have to move very carefully! If they find out we have this negative, they'll probably just kill us for it."

"What do we do now?" Lauren cried.

"What can we do?" Midge sighed. "Except wait."

Midge sat down and lit a cigarette. "I hate to wait," she said, to no one in particular.

The three felt silent. Suddenly a little ball of fur came hurtling out of the hole in the wall.

"Oh, no, The note's still there!" Jackie cried. "We didn't contact Velma."

"Not so fast," said Midge, taking the note from Jackie. While there was no added writing, the word "Kitty" had been carefully torn from the paper.

"We've reached Velma!" Midge cried.

"How do you know?" asked Jackie and Lauren.

"We saw this in an old movie one night; the heroine had no pen, so she ripped a part of the message instead to let her rescuers know she was still alive."

"Now that we know she's alive, all we have to do is find her," Midge declared.

But their continued search for a way out was futile. They finally agreed to get some sleep, taking turns staying awake in case any of their jailers decided to pay them a visit.

"I wonder what Cherry's doing right now," Midge sighed, staring at the full moon. "I sure hope she's having a better time than we are."

"Could there be a worse time than this?" Lauren sighed dramatically.

Jackie started to laugh. "Yes, there is a worse time than this, and her name is Trixie."

"Not Trixie with the poodles!" Midge cried.

"Oh, no! You, too?"

Lauren grumbled and turned over. She had no idea what they were talking about, and she was frankly too exhausted to care! When she fell asleep five minutes later, Midge and Jackie were still laughing.

Midge's turn as sentry came as the sun was rising. She had slept badly on the cold stone floor, and she was hungry, but all she could think of was her beloved Velma.

"Soon we'll be together again," she prayed. She stroked the tiny mouse, asleep in her palm, and watched the sun rise.

Without warning the door swung open, and two deacons stormed in. One of them was armed with a rifle!

Midge jumped up. "Aren't you boys a little old to be playing dress-up?" she taunted the men.

"Shut up!" the gunman cried. His partner grabbed Midge, who could have overpowered the man had she not had a gun pointed at her head.

The gunman suddenly shrieked. "I've been bitten," he

cried, dropping his gun and grabbing his right ankle.

"Aargh!" he screamed, grabbing his other foot. "I've been bitten again."

Midge threw his partner against the stone wall, knocking him cold. Within seconds the girls had jumped the gunman.

Midge pointed the gun at his head. "Tell us where you've got the girl," she demanded.

"She's in the boiler room," the man blurted out, before fainting from fear.

"I'd just as soon kill these guys," Midge said. "But we might need them later," she pointed out. "We might not be able to find Velma all by ourselves."

"Good thinking," Jackie agreed. "Let's tie them up. Drat! They took our rope away from us last night, remember?"

Midge's eyes lit up. "I almost forgot—I've got handcuffs in my pocket!"

She expertly cuffed the men together. "There, these boys won't be going anywhere soon," she said. She held up the little key she kept on a chain around her neck.

"Gee, hope I don't lose this," she said sarcastically, tossing it out the window. "Darn shame to waste a good pair of cuffs on these losers," Midge said ruefully.

"Don't worry," Jackie consoled Midge. "When we get back to the city, I'll get you another pair—government issue."

The little brown mouse sat atop the deacons, chattering her teeth.

"What's she trying to say?" asked Jackie.

"That's how mice laugh," Midge explained.

The mouse kept chattering, causing the three girls to break out in giggles, which they tried to suppress.

"Shhh," said Jackie. "There's at least three more of these guys, remember? Not to mention that jerky altar boy we met out front."

The girls stifled their laugher, but the stone corridors continued to echo.

"Why, that sounds like the laughter of children," Jackie gasped. "Could it be that Father Helms is so dastardly that he's holding children hostage, too?"

CHAPTER 19

An Unfortunate Slip

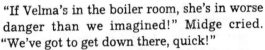

"If Velma's in the boiler room, she's in worse danger than we imagined!" Midge cried. "We've got to get down there, quick!"

Midge raced into a long dark corridor with rows of identical doors, Lauren and Jackie following close behind her.

"This is so creepy," Lauren shivered, peeking through the windows of the cells. "They're all the same," she declared. "I can't believe anyone used to live here!"

"I remember there was a stone staircase at the end of a corridor on the eastern side of the building that led down to the lower levels," Midge explained. "But I was so dizzy after that priest slugged me, I lost my sense of direction coming in.

"Sister Agnes once explained to me that these corridors are built in the shape of a cross. We're right at the intersection. We have to figure out which way is east."

Lauren pulled a compass from her pocket and checked their position. "We should head that way!" she pointed.

"Under the convent are hot mineral springs," Midge explained as the three hurried down the corridor. "In the late 1930s, Sister Julia, who was particularly adept at engineering, figured out a way to run the steam through pipes, thus heating the entire convent. The door is always kept securely locked; only qualified nun technicians are allowed to go down there.

"Why, the water is so scalding, it would take a miracle for someone to survive a plunge in it," Midge shivered.

"Look!" Jackie said. They had found the staircase, but their exit was blocked by an iron-bar door, which had been padlocked shut.

Luckily, the keys they had taken from the two deacons,

who now lay cuffed together in the girls' cell, opened the rusty padlock!

In a flash the three girls were running down the white stone staircase, following the spiraling path down, down, down. Electric lights had been hung at intervals along the crumbly dirt walls.

The stairs emptied into a well-lit cellar that had large wooden shelves along one wall and low sinks lining another. The shelves were filled with dozens of jars of fruit. In the middle of the room was an old oak work table, scarred with many years' use.

"This is where the nuns do their canning," Midge whispered, keeping her voice low in case the enemy was nearby.

Jackie spied an open jar of pears on the counter next to the sink. "Someone's been here recently for a snack," she said, upon examining the jar. The fruit seemed fresh, and not at all spoilt.

The sound of footsteps heading their way startled the girls. "We've got to hide!" Jackie whispered, gesturing toward a large wardrobe at the far end of the room. But, hard as they tried, they couldn't get the old cabinet open. And the footsteps were getting closer!

"I know where we can hide," Midge whispered urgently. "The laundry room!" She pulled her chums through a curtain at the back of the room. The smell of starch hung in the air. Neatly folded linens and freshly starched wimples were stacked on a table. In the middle of the room was a large chute that came out of the ceiling and emptied into an enormous hamper.

"Jump in!" Midge whispered urgently. The three girls climbed over the side and disappeared into a sea of black serge habits.

Lauren wanted to giggle when she came up for air. Something about being in a sea of habits struck her as funny, but she changed her mind when Jackie put a cautionary finger to her lips. Someone was in the next room!

They listened with bated breath while someone rummaged through the jars of food. "All day long, it's fetch this and fetch that," a boy was complaining to himself.

"It's the altar boy," Jackie said in a low tone. Jackie looked at the disgusted expression in Midge's eyes and knew they were thinking the same thing. They should have eliminated him when they had the chance!

They held their breath until they heard the altar boy go back up the stairs. Jackie and Midge leapt out of their hiding place, but had to help Lauren, who had become tangled in the heap of clothing and emerged with her head through the neck of a nun's habit.

"These horrible habits are so darn itchy," she declared, struggling free of the confining outfit. "No wonder my teachers are always so crabby with me."

"That must be it," Midge said dryly. "Now, let's go!" She led them back through the main room. "Figures, he didn't clean up after himself," Midge sneered. She vowed that when this was all over she'd personally teach that boy some manners!

"Now, if I remember correctly, the boiler room is through this door and down a tunnel," she said, heading toward a dark corner underneath the stairway.

"Oh no, the door's been wrenched open. He must be down there with Velma right now," she said, ducking through the small stone portal. Lauren and Jackie shivered as they found themselves in a dark, damp tunnel.

The girls crept single-file over the hard dirt floor, guided only by Lauren's dwindling supply of matches. Suddenly Midge halted the procession. They could see a sliver of light shining through the slightly open door ahead. She signaled the girls to stop.

"Be very quiet," she said in a voice so low it was barely a whisper. "I'll go ahead. You two stay here until I give a signal that I need your help. Give me the gun, Jackie."

Jackie hesitated. She felt she should be the one to go in first. After all, she was a police officer and knew how to handle this kind of dangerous situation. But she also knew that she'd get nowhere arguing with Midge, who'd do anything to save Velma.

She reluctantly handed Midge the gun. She only hoped she was making the right decision!

Midge leaned close to Jackie's ear. "If Velma and I don't make it, take Lauren and scram.There's an escape hatch right under the hamper we were hiding in. It leads to the underground rooms; they're probably holding the nuns there." She gave Jackie a swift hug and patted Lauren on the head.

Midge crept the few last feet to the boiler room, and cautiously peeked though the crack in the open door.

There was Velma, bound to a chair, and leaning over her in a menacing manner was the evil priest, Father Helms.

And right behind them was the bubbling pool of scalding water! Would it be Velma's final resting place?

Midge stuck the gun in her belt, and cautiously pushed open the door, praying that the priest wouldn't notice the door creaking.

"It's about time you boys got here," Father Helms hissed, his back still to Midge.

"Lucky break," Midge thought. "Those dumb deacons are good for something after all." She crept across the floor.

Edging into the room, Midge took the gun from her belt and aimed at the priest. "The minute he moves away from Velma, he's a dead man," she thought, wiping sweat from her brow.

"I can't get this damn girl to talk," the priest scowled, glaring daggers at Velma. "Perhaps one of her little friends would like go for a swim. Then maybe she'll remember where she hid that negative," he cackled, turning toward what he thought were his cohorts. His smile crumbled when he found himself looking down the barrel of a gun.

"Don't shoot!" he cried, grabbing the back of Velma's chair and tipping her dangerously near the bubbling pool of scalding water. "If I go down, she goes with me," he hissed. "Hand over the gun."

"No...no," Midge said, her voice trailing off into a little sob. She laid her gun on the floor, and kicked it over to the priest. He let go of the chair and picked up the gun. He pointed it straight at Midge.

"You have the wrong girl there," Midge cried. "*I've* got what you want."

"Where is it?" the priest cried, his eyes narrowing with suspicion.

"First, let her go," Midge demanded.

"Not until you show me the negative," the priest cried, his voice shaking with rage.

"I have it in safekeeping with a friend," Midge said. "If you let Velma go, I'll lead you right to it." She could tell he didn't believe her, so she described the negative to him.

"It'll look great on the front page of every newspaper in

America," she added. "Which is where it will be if we don't get out of here alive.

"I'll lead you to it, but only if you let the girl go!" she repeated. "You and I will walk out of here together."

Beads of sweat appeared on the priest's upper lip. His eyes darted back and forth nervously. "He looks like a cornered rat," thought Midge, "only not so intelligent."

"Midge, if you don't make it, I don't want to either," Velma cried. "I couldn't bear life without you!"

"My, what a touching little scene," the priest cooed viciously.

"He'll shoot you for sure, once he gets what he wants. Why, I overheard him say he's going to blow up the convent!" Velma burst into tears.

"Shut up, you," the priest cried, smacking Velma across her pretty face.

Midge forgot all about the gun pointed straight at her and lunged at the evil priest. She grabbed him around his scrawny neck and squeezed with all her might. The strong girl shook the man to and fro, squeezing his neck until his eyes threatened to pop out of his face. His arms flailed about like a rag doll's. The gun went off.

Velma screamed. "Behind you, Midge! Someone's been shot!"

"Oh, my god, Lauren!" Jackie cried.

Midge released her hold on the priest, who slumped to the ground gasping for air. A look of despair crossed Midge's face when she saw the limp figure of the girl sprawled across the doorway. She raced to her side.

Jackie knelt over Lauren's body. "We were just rushing in to help, and she took a bullet in the chest," she cried, checking Lauren's pulse. "She's still alive, but her pulse is faint!"

"Such a sweet kid," Midge murmured.

"Midge! Look out!" Velma cried.

But they were too late, for the evil priest had recovered, and was advancing on the girls. In his shaky hand was the gun!

"Now you're all my prisoners," he growled, rubbing the bruises on his throat. "I don't believe you've hidden that negative. Hand it over."

But Midge refused. She knew that their only chance of staying alive would be to hang on to that negative!

Just then an altar boy sporting a black eye hobbled in, carrying a tray of food. "I've got your stewed prunes, Father," he said. He hopped over Lauren's body, put down the tray and made a face at the girls. "These are the nasty girls who beat me up," he whined.

"Search her," the priest commanded, pointing to Midge.

The boy complied without a word. Midge grimaced as she felt his slimy hands running over her body. He found the envelope containing the negative in the right heel of Midge's sturdy black loafer.

The priest examined the negative carefully. "This is it," he cried, jigging for joy. He cackled with delight as he danced over to the pool and dropped the negative in.

"Now that I've discovered where those crazy nuns hid that body, thanks to you girls, all the evidence is destroyed. Get up against that wall—now!" he snapped, waving toward the wall with his gun.

"And you," he said, pointing to the altar boy. "Get that body out of the doorway. And then scram."

Tears filled Jackie's huge black eyes when she saw Lauren's limp body being dragged across the floor.

"You'll never get away with this," Jackie threatened.

"Sure I will. It's all worked out just the way I planned."

He related a tale so ghastly the girls gasped in horror. The more he talked the giddier he got, until the girls knew every gruesome detail of his fiendish plot.

"When Bishop Clarence ordered me to seize this land, I thought it would be a simple matter of getting rid of the Mother Superior. But it wasn't that simple. I discovered that instead of naming the church as beneficiary, as good nuns do, she willed all her property to some damn woman!

"I had to have this land!" he shrieked. "The Bishop said if I took care of this, I'd go all the way to Rome!"

"So one day I followed your Mother Superior on one of her many trips to San Francisco. I followed her to Lindy Lane, where I overheard her discussing plans to renovate the underground rooms of the convent with her friend Gertrude— that nosy dame who's been hanging around here for years. I should have put a stop to that long ago," he grumbled.

"They're both down there now," he gloated.

"I broke into her house and found all the evidence I needed to implicate these nuns in the biggest kidnapping ring of the century. It will be quite a feather in my cap to find all those missing wives and children!

"You should have seen her expression when I told her I was going to inform the authorities of the devilish activities going on here! She promised me she would pack and go, and sign over the land to me, too.

"But then my beautiful plan was foiled by some nun with a camera. That murder wasn't even my fault," he complained. "I struck out in self-defense to keep that nosy accountant from the Catholic Men's Club from going to the police with his little story of embezzlement.

"I was trapped! What could I do? I had already told the Bishop the land was practically mine! Then that damn Mother Superior skipped town with the negative, but I got her back. I had to kidnap a few more nuns than planned, but now I've finally got the negative back, too.

"We've been trying to tame this bunch of nuns for a long time, and we're finally going to succeed. Ha, ha, ha!" he laughed victoriously. He backed toward the door, his gun trained on the girls. "I've got a bomb hooked up in the bell tower. When the bell chimes three o'clock, it will detonate, and this place will be blown to smithereens!

"I'd shoot you now, but I think you'll want to use this last bit of time to reflect upon your sins," he sneered.

Suddenly, as if out of nowhere, Cherry Aimless came hurtling through the open doorway, knocking the priest so hard that he flew right into the deadly pool!

"Golly," she cried, racing to the edge of the pit and reaching out a helping hand. "Don't worry, I'm a nurse."

"Don't save him!" Midge cried. "He imprisoned your aunt and countless other women!"

Cherry searched her heart, but she could find no compassion for this man. She snatched away her outstretched hand and the priest slipped into the steamy abyss.

Quick as a flash Midge untied Velma, who fell into her arms. "I can't believe he killed that little girl," she sobbed.

"I am not a little girl," Lauren hollered. She sat straight up. "And I'm not dead either!" She pulled the stuffed bear out of the front pocket of her overalls. "Billy took the bullet for me," she said solemnly, pointing to a hole in the bear's head.

Jackie swept Lauren up in her strong arms and exclaimed, "You are one lucky little punk." Lauren squirmed in embarrassment. "Put me down," she demanded, secretly pleased by the attention.

"I'll never make fun of that stupid bear again," Midge said solemnly.

Lauren rubbed a bruise on her temple. "I must have knocked myself out when I hit the floor," she said. "What's going on?"

"All this is a mystery to me, too!" Cherry cried.

"Good work, Cherry," Jackie beamed. "Your timing was perfect."

"Is this who I think it is?" Jackie asked, reaching out to shake hands with the titian-haired stranger at Cherry's side.

Midge slapped Cherry on the back after Nancy introduced herself. "Good work!" she cried. "You're a better detective than I thought.

"We've all got a lot of explaining to do," Midge added, "but first we've got to disarm a bomb and free some nuns. Does anyone besides me know how to dismantle an explosive?" They all shook their heads.

"They don't allow girls on the Bomb Squad," Jackie said. She laughed. "I think they're afraid to let girls learn too much about bombs."

"I'll have to do it, and the rest of you will have to find the nuns."

"And there are more armed deacons somewhere in the convent," Jackie added. "So we're not out of danger yet."

"But I don't know anything about capturing criminals," Cherry protested.

"I do," Nancy volunteered, remembering that in *The Case of The Twice-Burnt Toast* she had overpowered a gang of criminals using just the contents of her purse.

"I'd better get to the bell tower," Midge said. Velma, refusing to be parted from Midge for another second, insisted she would accompany her on her mission.

"And the rest of us will find the nuns and free them! But no matter what, we all have to be out of here within twenty minutes," Jackie said sternly.

Everyone agreed, and after synchronizing their watches to Cherry's sturdy nurse's watch, the girls hurried out of the boiler room to complete their dangerous assignments.

CHAPTER 20

The Countdown Begins

Midge led them back into the cellar. "Remember what I told you earlier about the tunnel under the hamper?" she said to Jackie. "That leads to underground rooms."

Cherry checked her watch. "Golly, we've got to hurry. There's only seventeen minutes left!" Midge grabbed Velma's hand and started up the spiral stone stairway.

"I've had lots of experience with tunnels," Nancy called up the stairs after her. "I feel confident that we can find our way."

Under Jackie's guidance, the girls pushed the heavy hamper aside. Jackie knelt down and rapped on the solid slab of stone underneath.

"This must lift up somehow," she said, feeling around the edges for a crack. She found a space big enough to put her fingers in, and after rolling up her sleeves, she lifted the slab out of their way. Cherry secretly thrilled at the sight of Jackie's powerful arms straining under the weight of the stone. Underneath was a chute, but it was too dark to see where it led!

Nancy fearlessly jumped into the chute.

"Oh, I hope I don't get too dirty," moaned Cherry, as she, too, lowered herself into the opening. Halfway down the chute she got stuck, and it took some pushing from Jackie to dislodge her. Cherry and Jackie tumbled through the duct, and landed together on the stone floor.

"Oh!" Cherry cried, struggling to pull down her skirt, which had flown up above her waist.

Jackie rolled off of her and grinned. "Let me get that for you, Cherry," she offered helpfully.

Cherry stood up and smoothed her skirt. "It's awfully warm in here!" she exclaimed, her face blazing with embarrassment.

Jackie rose to her feet just in time to catch Lauren before she hit her head for the second time that day. The girl had impetuously jumped head-first through the chute.

"Hey, look!" Lauren cried.

For there in the corner sat Nancy Clue, with the three armed deacons bound and gagged at her feet!

"Wow!" Jackie cried. "Some day you've got to show me how you did that so fast."

"Oh," Nancy said modestly, "it was nothing."

Cherry checked her watch. "We must hurry," she urged. "Time's running out." The girls rushed off down a brightly-lit passage. No more than a dozen feet into their journey, they were surprised to find the tunnel split off in two directions.

"Midge didn't say anything about a fork in the road!" Nancy cried. "This must be a recent addition." She put her finger to her pretty face and frowned. "Let's see. There was a tunnel in *The Case of the Lingering Lilies*. I got trapped in one. Why, I would have perished had my little dog Gogo not alerted my chums Bess and George to my whereabouts!

"I stayed in that tunnel for three days before being freed. Luckily I had a loaf of bread, chocolate bars, oranges and some milk in my purse," she recalled. "But that's really of no help to us," she added sadly.

"Would this help?" Cherry said brightly, pulling out the map she had found in Aunt Gert's secret room. "I was just fishing through my purse for some chewing gum when I found it. It could be a map of these tunnels."

Nancy's bright blue eyes flashed with delight. "This has got to be it," she said, after examining the piece of paper in Cherry's hand.

"Yes, look. On this map, the tunnel leading to the dormitory branches off to the left," Jackie pointed out. "Let's go!" she said, leading the way down the path.

Lauren trotted along eagerly behind her.

Cherry slipped out of her heels. "It's so much easier now to walk," she sighed.

Nancy put her arm around Cherry's shoulder. "And now you're a perfect fit," she murmured.

"This must be it," Jackie called back to them.

"Yeah, hurry up, you two," Lauren added, holding open a door at the end of the tunnel.

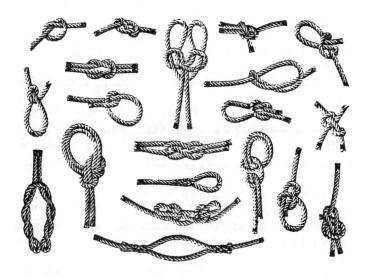

"Why, it looks like people live down here all the time!" Cherry cried. Toys and books were scattered everywhere among the neat rows of narrow beds. The cold stone floor had been made more cheerful by the addition of thick rag rugs.

Cherry exclaimed over the unusual statues set into nooks in the wall.

"They're the ancient goddesses," Lauren explained, adding that she was studying mythology in school. "Why would a bunch of nuns have statues like these?" she wondered.

"No one's here," Cherry frowned. "But there are signs of life everywhere," she said, pointing to the clothing lying on the beds. Cherry was frankly scared. According to her watch, they had just twelve minutes left!

"Somewhere there's got to be a way through here," Cherry said, frantically passing her hands over the stone wall in a vain attempt to find loose stones that might indicate a secret entry.

Suddenly, she gasped in horror.

"Oh, no!" Cherry cried. "I broke a nail!"

"Those nails have got to go," her titian-haired chum

whispered. "I was going to talk to you about them later."

"There's got to be another hiding place," Lauren said determinedly, looking under the beds for the entryway to another tunnel. When she couldn't find one, she ran to a shelf and started yanking books from it.

"What are you doing?" Nancy gasped.

"Looking for a secret door," Lauren said. "You got a better idea?"

Nancy rolled her eyes. "You girls read too many detective stories when you were kids," she said, going over to the far wall and pulling aside a heavy tapestry. "How about through there?" she asked, pointing to a thick wooden door behind it.

Lauren looked chagrined and ran to the door. But it was locked! Nancy called out, but there was no answer. "This place is going to blow!" she yelled, but there was still no answer.

Jackie deftly produced the deacons' keys and quickly unlocked the door, which flew open to reveal Gertrude Aimless in a nun's habit!

"Oh, Aunt Gert!" Cherry sobbed, falling into her arms.

"Cherry, I knew you'd come; I prayed for you to rescue us!" her aunt cried back, covering Cherry's wet cheeks with kisses.

"I don't want to break up this happy scene, but we've got to move quickly!" Jackie exclaimed.

Cherry checked her watch. "Aunt Gert, we've got only seven minutes left before a bomb explodes. We've got to get out!"

Gert turned back into the cluttered storage room, stacked high with old furniture. She clapped her hands smartly, and from the shadows emerged more nuns than Cherry had ever seen before, each with a makeshift weapon in hand. Behind them were many women and children.

"What did you do with the deacons?" Aunt Gert wondered aloud. Jackie quickly explained the fate of the men, and a sunny grin broke over Aunt Gert's handsome face.

"Let's go," said Gert, waving them forward in her best military manner. The nuns were a blur to Cherry as they raced out of the room, through the dormitory and to the tunnel.

"We'll never make it," Cherry cried. "Why, all these people have to get back to the cellar and climb up that chute. It will take forever!" she exclaimed.

"Nonsense," her aunt said briskly.

"There's an escape tunnel to the outdoors," Nancy guessed. "At any rate, there was one in *The Secret of the Shivering Sheltie.*"

"Bingo!" Aunt Gert cried. Cherry blushed. She felt like a silly goose for losing her head that way. Nancy saw her consternation and gave her chum a little squeeze.

"Follow me," Aunt Gert directed, as she raised her habit high above her ankles and ran.

"The other branch of the tunnel leads to the outdoors," she called out over her shoulder. Cherry checked her watch as she hurried to catch up to the nuns. Only three minutes remained!

They raced around the corner and started down the right-hand tunnel. Cherry gripped Nancy's hand. Would they make it in time?

"We're here!" Aunt Gert called out. With Jackie's help, she moved a circular stone from the wall. Cherry could see daylight at the end of a long escape hatch. One by one the women and children passed through the pipe, which emptied out onto the banks of a river. Soon they were all in the brilliant sunshine, surrounded by the sweet scent of lavender, which grew wild around the convent.

Cherry checked her watch and gasped. Where were Midge and Velma? They had only one minute left!

CHAPTER 21

Just in Time!

"I'm going back in," Jackie said, starting for the convent.

"No!" Cherry said firmly, surprising everyone with her vehemence. "We've got to trust them; we can't risk losing you—not after all this." Cherry threw her arms around Jackie. She looked frightened.

Nancy looked a little jealous.

Jackie looked grim. "How long?" she asked.

"Thirty seconds."

They held their collective breath.

Cherry began the countdown. "twenty-nine...twenty-eight...twenty-seven..." Suddenly, her sturdy nurse's watch stopped ticking. She shook it, but it was dead.

"This wasn't supposed to happen!" Cherry cried. "It has a lifetime guarantee."

Nancy had been counting under her breath, and she raised her voice so the others could hear. "twenty seconds...nineteen...eighteen...seventeen..."

Many of the nuns were holding hands and praying.

"seven...six...five...four...three...two..."

"Oh, please let Midge and Velma be safe," Cherry prayed.

"One!"

Silence.

The building was still standing!

The tower bell began to peal madly.

"Look," cried Jackie, "Midge is ringing the bell!"

Like an actor in a swashbuckler movie, Midge grabbed Velma with one arm and, using the bell rope, shimmied down the convent wall. Everyone ran to greet them, cheering madly.

"You did it!" cried Cherry, hugging Midge and Velma.

"You did it, too!" Midge cried, nodding toward the rescued women and children.

"And Nancy tied up three deacons all by herself," Cherry boasted, hugging her new chum. Nancy blushed and introduced herself to everyone.

"Did you really overpower the deacons all by yourself?" Midge asked. Cherry could see Midge had new respect for the girl sleuth.

Nancy laughed. "What I want to know is where you learned how to disarm that bomb."

Midge grinned. "I took a class when I was in the state, ah, university," she chuckled, adding, in a more serious tone, "We got there just in time. For a moment there, I thought we weren't going to make it. When we got to the top of the building, we lost our perspective and didn't know which way to turn to get to the bell tower room."

Cherry gasped. "How horrible," she said. "How did you find your way in there?"

Midge gently reached into her breast pocket and pulled out the little brown mouse. "This little angel," she said. "Later I'm going to find a nice big piece of cheese for her."

This gave Aunt Gert an idea. "All this excitement's made me hungry; let's go and have a nice big meal, and I'll explain everything. I've got a lot to tell you, Cherry," she said, as she herded the group toward the convent.

"We've got a few things to reveal, too," Midge said, taking Velma by the hand.

"And I can't wait to hear how you found Nancy Clue, Cherry," Jackie added, hurrying to catch up to the girl and her aunt.

Cherry blushed. "First," she said, "I've simply got to freshen up."

She went up to a pretty nun with pale skin and sparkling blue eyes, and asked if she could use her powder room. Something about the nun looked familiar. Cherry knew she had seen those eyes before, but where?

The nun gave Cherry a penetrating look, and grinned.

"Hello, Nurse Aimless," she said, in a familiar voice. The nun whipped off her wimple and fluffed her blond hair. "That's better," she grinned, laughing in that sparkling way that had haunted so many nurses' dreams.

"Lana!" Cherry cried. "You're a nun? What are you doing here?"

The nun giggled. "I've got someone who wants to see you," she laughed, pulling Cherry in the direction of a nun. She tapped the sister on the shoulder, and when Cherry saw who it was, she gave a little shriek.

"Head Nurse Marstad! What are you doing here?"

Then Cherry did what any girl would have done. That is, any girl who had been through what she had in the last twenty-four hours. She fainted!

CHAPTER 22

A Sumptuous Banquet

When she awoke a few hours later, Cherry found herself lying on a small cot with a cold compress on her head. An elderly nun was bending over her. "How do you feel, dear?" she asked, taking Cherry's hand in her small, soft one. Cherry tried to focus. "I'm all right," she said weakly, trying to get her dizzy thoughts together. The last thing she remembered was the sight of Nurse Marstad in a nun's habit.

"Is everyone a nun?" she wondered.

Aunt Gert appeared at the door. She had shed her habit for more casual attire.

"Are you strong enough to join us for dinner, dear, or should I bring a tray to your bed?" she asked.

"I think I can make it," Cherry replied, getting to her feet. "I feel fine now," she said, "only I'm still so confused. But I can't possibly dine in this outfit." She looked ruefully at her rumpled skirt.

Aunt Gert had to laugh at her neat niece. "You look fine," she said heartily. "Why, look at me."

Cherry did, as if for the first time. Aunt Gert was wearing a simple slacks and sweater outfit, with only a gold ring for adornment. Cherry smiled. "I guess it's come as you are," she said gaily.

"That's the spirit," Aunt Gert said. "You come and have a nice dinner, and afterward we'll explain everything to you."

Aunt Gert led her to a banquet room, with old tapestries on the wall and fine china set out on the table. Cherry admired the smiling faces of the women and children seated around the enormous oak table. She waved at Nurse Marstad, who was seated at the far end of the table, next to Jackie. They seemed to be engrossed in conversation. Cherry noticed Nurse Marstad looked all aglow. Was it the wine, she wondered? Jackie seemed particularly animated, too.

"It's nice to see two people I like getting along so well," she thought, noting that Nurse Marstad looked particularly fetching in her snug coral cashmere sweater. Why, Cherry had never seen her looking quite so lovely!

Cherry settled shyly in the seat next to Nancy. "I'm so glad you're okay," Nancy whispered, squeezing her hand. Cherry just blushed.

Aunt Gert settled at one end of the long table; Lana was at the other. "We've already had our soup, but we saved the blessing for you," Gert said, bowing her head. They all joined hands.

Each woman in turn said what she was grateful for. When it was Cherry's turn, she was almost too overwhelmed to speak. "Why, I have so much to be thankful for!" she finally blurted out. "There's Midge and Velma, Aunt Gert and," a special tone crept into her voice, "and you, Nancy."

"Oh, don't go and get mushy on us, Cherry," Lauren broke in. "I'm starving. Let's eat." Everyone laughed, and dinner began.

"Is this what they call vegetarian?" Cherry wondered, surprised that vegetables could be so good. She made a mental note to pass on her mother's delicious green bean and potato chip casserole recipe to the chef.

"Gee, a family dinner with no fighting," Midge whispered to Velma. "Imagine that."

Velma placed her hand on Midge's thigh and squeezed. "Don't eat too much, honey," she said. "I don't want you to get too sleepy."

Midge grinned. "There's no way I'm going to fall asleep tonight," she promised.

Cherry saw the look that passed between the two girls. The sight of Velma and Midge together again warmed her heart. Tears of happiness welled up in her eyes. She knew her makeup would run, but she didn't care.

The meal continued, with dish after delicious dish being brought out from the kitchen by nuns wearing starched aprons over their tidy habits.

"Every nun's got her job here," Aunt Gert explained. "Sister Catherine MacCaffry, who you know as Lana, is the Mother Superior of this gang."

Cherry giggled at that. "Imagine calling an order of nuns a gang!" she thought.

"Sister Honey plans all our delicious meals. Her real name's Sister Edwina Ennis, but years ago some novice nun nicknamed her Honey, and it's stuck." Everyone said hello to the rubenesque nun wearing the stiff chef's hat.

Aunt Gert quickly introduced all the dinner guests. Cherry was surprised to find the convent had a Physical Education nun, as well as a nun whose single duty it was to train the convent's collies.

She was interrupted by a shy nun who whispered in her ear.

"The police are here," Lana said. "Will you excuse me for a moment?"

When she returned, she was all smiles. "Everything has been taken care of," she announced. "The deacons have been removed for good by our friend on the force. Officer Hillary Hinton sends her regards. She says not to worry about a thing."

After everyone had eaten their fill, Aunt Gert asked the girls to join her in her sitting room.

"Our visitors and I haven't had a moment to talk. Will you excuse us from chores this one time?" she asked the others at the table. Everyone nodded.

Cherry was so excited she could hardly keep still one minute longer. "I've just got to know everything. I've been trying to figure it all out in my head, but nothing makes sense!" she cried as she followed the others into the comfortable sitting room, attractively furnished with overstuffed chairs and flowered chintz curtains.

"Lana...I mean, Mother Superior, how did you get to my hospital? And, Aunt Gert, how do you know Lana...er, Mother Superior? Oh golly, my head's all dizzy!" she cried, collapsing onto a chair. Her face was flushed with excitement.

Aunt Gert went over to her befuddled niece and smoothed her short curly hair, so much like her own. Just as she was about to speak, there was a knock at the door. It was Sister Kimi, the dessert nun. "I thought you'd all like some sweets," said the adorable nun, pushing a tray filled with mouth-watering cookies and cakes. Cherry noticed she was wearing a habit that came to well above her shapely knees.

"We've got a lot to explain to Cherry. Let's all get comfortable first." Aunt Gert cut thick slices of scrumptious-looking coconut cake and passed them around. Midge licked the icing from her fingers. In fact, she licked Velma's fingers, too!

The Mother Superior cuddled up on the couch next to Aunt Gert, balanced her china cup on her knee, and smiled shyly at Cherry.

"Yes, Cherry, I'm your mysterious amnesia victim. In fact everyone calls me Lana now.

She continued. "This property belongs to me. It's been in my family for generations, but since I'm the last one in my line, when I die the church stands to inherit it.

"Years ago, I decided to join this order because of all the good they do for women and children. My aunt was the Mother Superior then, and she's the one who put the secret underground tunnels to use, helping women and children in trouble run away to better lives."

"That's what those are used for! What a great idea!" Cherry cried.

Lana continued her story. "Ten years ago I secretly drew up another will, leaving everything to Gert. We went on with our lives as usual, growing grapes for wine, teaching at the girls' school in town, faking passports and birth certificates for the women and children who depend on us to help them escape their brutal husbands."

"Wow!" Cherry cried. "And I thought I had a busy life!"

"We could use a nurse," Aunt Gert joked. "Ever thought about becoming a nun?"

"I think it's too late for that," Cherry blushed, glancing at Nancy.

Lana went on with her story. "A few months ago, several attempts were made on my life. At first I thought it was just a series of mishaps, but when the brakes on my car went out for a third time, I knew someone was after me!"

"When I heard through the grapevine that Father Helms had been instructed by Bishop Clarence to take away our land and build a retirement home for priests on it, I knew he was behind all the accidents. I've always known that man was ruthless, but I had no idea he would actually murder to get what he wanted!" she shuddered.

"I told him the Church was no longer in my will. The accidents stopped.

"I thought I had managed to stave him off, but then the day of the All Saint's Carnival, held every year on the convent grounds, I read a newspaper story announcing that ground would be broken soon for the new retirement home for priests—and at the site of the *former* Sisters of Mercy convent!

"When I confronted Father Helms, he waved a piece of paper in my face and laughed. He had broken into my safe and stolen my map of the tunnel. He laughed as he taunted me with it. He said the tunnels would make great bowling alleys," she shivered.

"I thought all was lost," she admitted. "We've broken a lot of laws over the years. Transporting minors across state lines, falsifying identification paper, things like that.

"He demanded that we turn the land over to him or we'd all be put in jail. I pretended to go along with him. I told him that we'd pack and leave in the morning. But in the back of my mind, I was planning a murder!

"I had decided that no matter what, I would save this place. Even if I had to drive a stake through his heart!" she said forcefully.

"That night the carnival happened as scheduled. The clean-up crew was comprised entirely of women who were going underground that night. We prepared their quarters and were busy putting the finishing touches on their paperwork when a novice nun, Sister Darlene, came running in. She announced that she had something very important for me to see!

"You see, Sister Darlene and Sister Drew were in charge of the photo booth. For a dollar, parishioners have their picture taken with a statue of the Madonna. It's very popular with our older ladies," she added.

"Well, these young nuns had taken a break and were fooling around out in the fields way beyond the convent proper. Sister Darlene was taking nature studies of Sister Drew when she happened upon a ghastly sight!

"Father Helms was dragging a dead man through the woods. She quickly snapped a photograph of it, hid behind a rock and watched as he buried the corpse. When the priest left, they unearthed it, and discovered it was Mr. Harry Harms, head of the Men's Catholic Club, the group in charge of the carnival. It was common knowledge that Father Helms had been siphoning funds from the group for years.

People let him do it; he was a powerful figure in this community.

"I guess he got a little too greedy. Mr. Harms must have confronted him, and paid for it with his life!

"When the sisters told me they had evidence linking the priest to the murder, I knew I had some leverage with him. But before I told him, we dug up the body and hid it, to keep him from doing away with it."

"So that's the body we found in the chapel," Lauren gasped. "The one I bumped into."

"That's when the priest caught us," Midge added.

"You found a dead body?" Cherry shrieked.

Lana continued. "I told Father Helms that at six a.m. mass the next day, he'd get what was his.

"You should have seen the grin on his face. He thought I meant I was turning over the convent," Lana giggled. "Boy, was he surprised the next morning when he saw photographic evidence of his crime.

"You see, we have a complete darkroom here," she added, "so we made a print of the negative and slipped into the chapel late that night and placed it in his hymnal.

"I didn't count on what happened next. He became so enraged he left the chapel right then and there and raced to his car. He was screaming that he would blow up the convent and be rid of us for good! I had hidden the negative in a book for safekeeping. I ran to my study and grabbed it, making sure he saw me leave. I knew he'd follow me; that's how I planned it.

"What I *didn't* plan on was getting kidnapped from the ward at Seattle General. Father Helms's right-hand man, Deacon McCarthy, snuck in, dressed as a nun. He had a gun and said he would shoot anyone who got in his way unless I came with him. When I left the ward, Father Helms was waiting for me in the hallway. When I saw they were driving Gert's car, I was terrified that his plans to blow up the convent had been carried out. They worked me over pretty good, but they couldn't find the negative."

"Because I had it all along," Cherry cried, finally beginning to make sense of the puzzle.

Lana nodded. "I never meant to put you and your friends in any danger, Cherry. All I know is, I was drugged and put in the trunk of Gert's car. When I awoke I was here.

"I was relieved to see Gert and all my sisters were still alive, but we were trapped in the underground dormitory, locked in by the deacons!"

"And those evil men were following me the entire time." Cherry put two and two together. "All because I had the book containing the negative. Nurse Marstad, how did you know to send it to Midge, though? You and Midge must know each other!" she guessed. "But how?"

Midge quickly filled Cherry in on her true identity.

"I read about you in one of my dad's detective magazines," Nancy chimed in. "I remember he said he felt lucky to have such a good girl for a daughter," she recalled.

"Let me get this right," Cherry said, a befuddled look on her face. "Nurse Marstad's not really Nurse Marstad, and you're not really Midge. *And* you're an escaped convict! Midge, you told me you met Velma in a library!" she cried.

"I did. It was a prison library," Midge grinned. "I spent five long miserable years in jail. Then one day I met this beautiful English teacher who had volunteered to teach composition to inmates."

Velma beamed. She put a hand on Midge's muscled thigh, and picked up the story.

"I noticed Midge right off the bat. Even in her plain blue cotton prison dress she was quite handsome," Velma said. "Soon I found myself looking forward to my classes at Girl's Prison. A little too much," she added. "Talk about picking someone who's totally unavailable."

Everyone laughed.

"This is so exciting," Cherry chirped.

"Although I don't know how she could have found me attractive in that darn dress." Midge said. "The clothes were killing me; I knew I couldn't spend the rest of my life in that getup. Nothing personal," she added, looking Cherry's way. Cherry took no offense. She knew now that dresses weren't for every girl.

"So we devised a plan to spring Midge," Velma explained. "I started taking a teacher's helper with me, a girl who looked a lot like Midge. One day while I was in the warden's office complaining about Midge and her attitude problem, Midge changed clothes with my chum, donned her glasses, and simply walked out of the prison. When I got back to the classroom, the other inmates tied us up, and we pretended Midge had overpowered us."

"And the officials never suspected you?" Cherry wanted to know.

"Not a thing. I am obviously much too prim and proper to ever participate in anything like a jail break," Velma said.

"You're just an old spinster school teacher," Midge joked.

"We moved to Warm Springs, and we've been together ever since."

Cherry wiped a tear from her eye. "Golly," she gulped. "This is the most romantic story I've ever heard!"

"How do you live without an identity?" Nancy wanted to know.

Midge shrugged. "Velma handles all the paperwork, like leases and stuff, and when I need some sort of identification, I just make it." She showed them a wallet full of convincing-looking I.D. cards. "The nuns taught me well," she grinned.

"You're a member of Police Benevolent League?" Jackie asked in amazement.

Midge laughed. "Not really," she said. "It just comes in handy sometimes."

"What a terrific story," Nancy exclaimed. "It would make a great book."

"Or a movie!" Cherry suggested. "I even met a movie star in the bar last night who could play you," she suddenly remembered.

"Yes, Miss Cherry Aimless, what about last night?" Midge wanted to know. "How *did* you find Nancy Clue?"

Cherry blushed and groped for words. What could she possibly tell them about last night?

Nancy swiftly saved the day. "Cherry is a very good sleuth," she said. "She operated as any top-notch detective would have. She asked a lot of questions and covered a lot of territory. After an exhaustive search, she put two and two together and tracked me down!"

Everyone was impressed with the clear-headed detective job their chum Cherry had done, and said so.

"But how on earth did you find us in that boiler room?" Velma wanted to know.

"Yeah, Cherry, you came just in the nick of time. You saved our lives!" Lauren cried. "How did you do it?"

Cherry couldn't lie to her chums. "It was because of Nancy," she said proudly. "When we got to the convent, that horrid altar boy was out front. Nancy had the bright idea for us to pretend to be tourists, so we walked right up to him and asked him all sorts of questions about the convent. He told us about the layout of the place, including the 'really keen' boiler room far underground."

She giggled. "Boy, was he ever surprised when Nancy slugged him in the head with her purse and then left him in a bush, all tied up with his own robe! Once we got inside, we raced to the cellar. We heard that loudmouth priest boasting about his plans, and as we were preparing an attack, I slipped and stumbled right through the doorway and smack into that priest!

"You see, I'm really wearing the wrong kind of shoes for traversing tunnels," she explained.

Nancy gasped. "We forgot all about the altar boy," she exclaimed. She raced to the window, and peered through the heavy curtains out at the bushes. "He's still there," she grinned.

"We'll have to call someone to come and get him. Some day," Midge cracked.

"Well, accident or no accident, you girls sure saved the day," Aunt Gert cheered. "Hip, hip, hooray!"

Everyone looked happy, except for Cherry. She had a peculiar look on her face. "There's just one thing that puzzles me," Cherry blurted out. "Oh, Aunt Gert, are you really a nun?"

Gert laughed. "No, honey, I'm not. But my girlfriend is."

CHAPTER 23

A Shocking Revelation

"Wait a minute," Cherry cried. "Nuns aren't allowed to date, are they?" Gert and Lana just laughed.

"How did you two meet?" Jackie wanted to know.

"We met ten years ago at a costume party at the What If Club," Gert replied. "It took Lana several days to convince me she was really a nun."

"Nuns go to bars?" Cherry asked in a shocked tone.

"Does the Pope know about this?" Lauren wondered.

"Oh, you young girls are such prudes," Aunt Gert giggled. "Nuns do a lot of things the Pope doesn't know about. The way I see it, if the Pope can wear a dress, I can wear these pants," she said.

They all had a good laugh. Lana continued her story.

"Gert and I met and knew instantly that we were meant for each other. We were married nine years ago, not in the eyes of the church, but in the eyes of God."

"Or, whoever," Aunt Gert added, picking up the story. "We were happy here, until this land struggle started. I was in San Francisco the morning Lana disappeared with the evidence of the priest's wrongdoings. I was sitting down to my first cup of coffee when two armed deacons burst into my house, threw me in my car and brought me here. I was beside myself with worry; no one knew where Lana had gone! They trapped us down in that underground room, with no way out! We spent most of our time in the storage room, trying to fashion makeshift weapons. We were preparing for an attack when you girls showed up and saved us."

"I shudder to think what would have happened if you girls hadn't come along," Aunt Gert added.

"What really impressed me, Nancy, is how you tied up

those deacons using only one short rope," Midge broke in.

Nancy explained that she had learned to tie fifty different knots in the Girl Scouts. "It's an old trick; with the right training anyone can do it," she said modestly. She agreed to give them all a little demonstration the next day.

Sister Kimi appeared at the door. "Telephone for Jackie," she announced.

When Jackie left the room, Midge leaned over and whispered something in Nurse Marstad's ear. Cherry couldn't make out what she was saying, but she could see that it made quite an impression on Nurse Marstad, who giggled and turned bright pink!

"What's going on?" Cherry cried. "There's still so much that's a mystery to me. I don't know why you're here, Nurse Marstad. Not that it's any of my business," she added hurriedly. She hadn't meant to sound so bossy!

Nurse Marstad grinned, showing off her darling dimples. "Call me Peg, Cherry. All my friends do."

Cherry gulped. Golly, friends with Nurse Marstad? It was more than she could have hoped for!

"I left the hospital immediately after I spoke with you. I knew all along who our amnesia patient was. I followed the deacons' trail back here, but was caught sneaking around the outside of the convent."

Jackie returned as Nurse Marstad was finishing her story. She balanced on the arm of the head nurse's chair.

"Good news, Midge," she announced. "You are no longer a wanted criminal."

"Hip, hip, hooray!" the gang proclaimed.

"And I am no longer a patrol officer," Jackie added.

"What?" Cherry cried, stunned to hear the news. "Why, you put your life on the line saving all these people, while the boys at the station were busy laughing off possible leads. That can't be!"

Jackie's broad grin told her she was putting them on. "I'm no longer a patrol officer because I'm now the first black female detective in the SFPD!"

"Yes!" Midge exclaimed. Everyone broke out in wild cheering. Everyone except Nurse Marstad, who planted a big kiss on Jackie's cheek.

"There's still so much I want to know," Cherry cried.

"Midge, you never told me why you carry those handcuffs. And, Velma, what about..." Cherry stifled a yawn. She hadn't gotten much sleep in the last few days.

Midge yawned, too. "I am *so* tired!" she exclaimed. She took Velma's hand. "Come on, honey, you look tired. Time for bed."

Velma, who frankly looked wide awake, yawned too.

Aunt Gert suggested they all get a good night's sleep and meet again in the morning for one of her famous brunches.

"Why, we've got a lot of time to get to know each other!" Lana declared, inviting them all to stay as long as they liked in the spacious and comfortable convent.

"Now that all the big mysteries are cleared up, I can finally sleep," Cherry declared as she began neatly stacking the dessert plates and coffee cups.

All the girls pitched in and got the job done quickly. Suddenly Nancy, who had said very little all evening, spoke up.

"As long as we're telling the truth..." she started, her face turning red and her voice trailing off into a whisper.

"What is it, Nancy?" Aunt Gert went to the trembling girl and put an arm around her.

"This is very difficult to talk about," Nancy said. "But I must do it!" Everyone sat down and patiently waited for Nancy to have her say.

Nancy was in tears, unable to speak. Cherry rushed to her side.

"If it's about your father and his murder, we know all about it," she declared, squeezing her chum's hand.

Nancy shook her head.

"No, no!" she cried. "You don't know! Nobody knows!"

"Tell us what happened," Aunt Gert said gently.

After a few minutes, Nancy regained her composure. What she said next startled even the most hardened of the group.

"My father was not killed by Hannah Gruel! It was *I* who shot him!" she declared.

Cherry could scarcely believe what she was hearing. "Nancy Clue, *you* killed your own father? But why?"

"He was a monster!" Nancy cried. "To other people he was a civic leader and a respected attorney and even kind to animals. But in his own home he was a bully!"

She told them the whole horrible story.

"My mother died when I was three. Hannah Gruel was like a mother to me. For several years, things were good. Father was gone a lot on business and Hannah and I became the best of chums. But as I entered my teens, Father began spending more and more time around the house.

"The first time I got involved in a case with him, he was so pleased! I thought perhaps he had been lonely all those years without Mother. He seemed so happy to have someone to share in his interests.

"But pretty soon he wanted my help on all his cases, especially after all the publicity we received as a father-daughter team. After a while I barely had time for school and friends of my own! He frightened my best chums Bess and George so much they stopped coming to the house.

"He became obsessed with my appearance, insisting I wear grown-up dresses and stylish hair-dos. After we'd fight he'd always buy me something big and flashy, like a new car. The neighbors thought he was the greatest!"

She hung her head. Her voice dropped to a whisper.

"When I was thirteen I started maturing; I was becoming a woman. It was then he..." Her voice grew grim.

She took a deep breath. "From that time on until the day I shot him, my father...well, he forced me to do things."

She started to sob. "It was as if I were his wife!" she gasped. "The whole world thought he was the best dad ever. No one would have ever guessed what really went on in that tidy house in the exclusive neighborhood of River Depths.

"When he started bothering me, he told me that if I told anyone he'd harm Hannah," Nancy sobbed. "So I kept it a secret. No one else knows it, but Mother died in an asylum," she said, "and he used to say I was crazy, just like her! And he'd add, 'I could have you put away, just like I did her!'

"One day I couldn't stand it anymore! Hannah was going to visit her sister Hattie for a month, and I just knew it would get worse with her gone. I broke down and told her, and when my father came home, she confronted him.

"She said she was going to tell everyone what he really was, but he just laughed. 'Who'd believe you over me?' he said." Nancy put her hands over her ears. "Oh," she cried. "I can still hear his laughter.

"When Hannah picked up the phone to call the police, he

pulled it out of the wall. I thought he was going to kill her, so I ran to the den and got one of his guns.

"'Father!' I screamed. He turned and faced me. I shot him right through the heart. He was dead before he hit the floor.

"Hannah begged me to let her say she did it, and I agreed. I was so scared and upset; I wasn't sure what I was doing! I packed some clothes, jumped in my car and headed west.

"She told me to forget and never tell anyone what had happened. But I can't."

Nancy wiped her face on a clean handkerchief from Cherry.

"You're safe now; that's what matters," Aunt Gertrude said, putting her arms around the sobbing girl.

"Am I?" Nancy asked no one in particular. "Now I know what I've got to do," she said, rising from her chair looking very determined.

"I've got to go back to River Depths and free Hannah—no matter what it takes!"

"And we'll go with you!" Midge said.

"That's right!" cried Jackie. "There's got to be some way to prove what kind of man your father really was."

"There were letters he wrote to me," Nancy said. "Disgusting things that would prove his nature beyond a shadow of a doubt. Those and the diary I kept. I left them in my room; I was in such a panic that I forgot to take them."

"We'll go back and get that evidence!" Velma cried.

"You're not alone, Nancy!" Jackie added, already planning the investigation. "Why, with those letters and your diary, we're sure to get Hannah released, and clear you, too."

Lauren pulled a pencil from her overalls and grabbed some paper from the desk. "Gather round, girls," she cried. "We need a plan!"

CHAPTER 24

Cornered

Aunt Gert interrupted the excited girls. "We can plan everything tomorrow, girls," she said. "Right now I think Nancy needs some rest." She escorted Nancy and Cherry to a charming bedroom and lit a fire in the fireplace facing the comfortable double bed.

"This is lovely!" Cherry exclaimed, looking around at the cozy bedroom which had been decorated in warm coral tones. Cherry recognized the old oak bed. Why, it was Grandma Aimless's. She found the place in the headboard where, as a child, she had carved her initials.

"C.A., R.N.," she read as she ran her hand over the deep marks in the wood. "Why even then I knew I'd be a nurse someday," she murmured.

While Nancy washed her face and scrubbed her teeth in the little bathroom adjoining the bedroom, Cherry changed into flannel pajamas and fuzzy slippers on loan from Aunt Gert.

Midge and Velma, clad in matching blue-checked pajamas, stopped in to say good-night. They expressed their concern about Nancy, and urged Cherry to awaken them if she needed anything.

Then Lauren appeared at the door, drowning in pajamas three times her size. Jackie was at her heels. "Great! You get to sleep with each other and I get stuck with the squirt," Jackie groaned.

"And you'd better not snore," Lauren warned her.

"I just know you're a cover hog," Jackie teased.

"I guess I'm the only one sleeping alone here," a soft voice teased. It was Nurse Marstad, clad in a luxurious green satin lounging robe that accentuated her large gray eyes.

Why, Cherry had never noticed before that under the confines of a stiffly-starched nurse's uniform was the voluptuous body of a glamorous woman!

163

Cherry wasn't the only one who had noticed.

"That's a crying shame," Jackie said huskily, as she let her eyes roam the length of the head nurse's shapely form.

The teasing stopped when Nancy appeared. She looked worn and pale and very tiny in her flannel pajamas. Her hair was brushed off her forehead. Her sky-blue eyes looked luminous against her pale skin.

Jackie hugged her goodnight. "If there's anything you need, just give a whistle."

Aunt Gert appeared at the door. Cherry giggled—she couldn't help herself. Aunt Gert looked so cute in her blue flannel pajamas and slippers. Using her best housemother voice, Gertrude Aimless shooed them all off to bed.

"I'll call you at five a.m. for morning mass," she called after them.

"Five a.m.!" they chorused in dismay.

Aunt Gert giggled. "Fooled you." Her laugh echoed down the hall.

The girls bade each other a hasty good-night. Nancy fell to sleep instantly, but Cherry lay awake, thinking of the horrible tale Nancy had told them. She tossed and turned for an hour, unable to sleep. Finally she put on her robe and slippers and crept quietly out of the room.

"If I can remember which room is the study, maybe I can find a good book and perhaps a piece of that delicious coconut cake to go with it," she thought.

She made her way down the hall and turned right. Or was the study on the left? Cherry was confused, and when she opened the door to what she thought was the study, she found herself in Midge and Velma's bedroom instead.

"Oops!" she cried.

Midge and Velma were wide awake, and their flannel pajamas were strewn about the floor. "You'll catch your death of cold in this drafty stone house," Cherry scolded.

Midge and Velma laughed, and promised they would put their pajamas back on soon. Cherry, satisfied that she would not have to worry about her chums, left to find the study.

A light under a distant door beckoned. "I'm earning my trailblazer badge for sure," Cherry smiled to herself. She quietly opened the door. She saw someone bending over Lana's desk. Cherry felt a chill run down her back—something was very wrong!

"Father Helms—you're alive," she gasped. Indeed, the evil priest was very much alive, and was at this very minute rifling through Lana's desk.

Cherry wanted to scream, but she was too frightened. She backed up, accidentally shutting the door behind her, trapping herself in the room.

The priest came toward her. His hands and face were badly burned; his clothes were in tatters. "You left me for dead in that steamy grave," he said hoarsely, walking ever closer toward the frightened nurse.

Cherry tried to speak; she tried to yell and warn the others, but she couldn't.

"No one imagined I could survive the intense heat, but I did! I clung onto a sharp rock in the side of the wall, and waited. Waited for all of you damn nuns to go to bed so I could exact my revenge! Perhaps with you as my prize, I'll get the deed to this land yet," he cackled.

Cherry gasped. She just couldn't be the reason Lana would lose her land. "Oh!" she cried, backing up. She groped behind her for something she could use as a weapon. Her hands closed on a statue. She yanked it off its pedestal and knocked the priest over the head with it.

The blow stunned him, but only temporarily. He kept coming at her.

So Cherry hit him again. And again. And again. His screams awoke the others, who came running. Aunt Gert, who reached the study first, gasped when she saw the battered priest lying on her good rug.

She quickly checked his pulse. "He's dead, all right!" she exclaimed.

"I can't believe I killed him!" Cherry cried, dropping the statue, which shattered into smithereens. "I didn't mean to kill him; I just meant to stop him."

The girls gathered round a shivering Cherry. Midge put her arm around the frightened nurse. "You're not taking all the credit for this, Cherry," Midge said. "The bubbling inferno should have finished him off, but I guess evil dies slowly." She took Cherry by the shoulders and looked her in the eyes. "Sometimes a girl's got to do what a girl's got to do," she declared.

Cherry blew her nose on a fresh handkerchief and nodded. Why, Midge was right.

"Think of all the women he hurt, Cherry. Why, it's as if you've saved all these people," Aunt Gert interjected.

"God knows what he would have done to us had you not stopped him," Lana said. "I would have done the same thing!"

"This is a clear case of self-defense," Jackie declared, covering the priest's body with her blue plaid bathrobe. "I'll call Hillary at the station and have this out of here in no time!"

Cherry suddenly felt very dizzy.

"Golly," she murmured, before fainting for the second time that day.

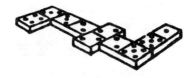

"I had a lot of time to think, what with the way that darn Lauren snores," she grinned. "I think we should all go to River Depths as soon as possible and get Nancy's diary and letters."

Midge nodded. "Velma and I had the same idea last night."

"Then Hannah will be free," Nancy said joyfully. Her smile turned into a frown. "I couldn't ask you to make that long trip just for me. Besides, when the news comes out, everyone in town will shun me. That won't be very pleasant for you. I think it's best if I go alone," she said mournfully. "I wouldn't want anything unpleasant to happen to any of you."

"Nonsense," the others chorused.

"You saved our lives," Velma said firmly. "Now it's time you let someone do something for you."

Cherry timidly put her hand in Nancy's. "I wouldn't dream of letting you go back alone to the place where those dreadful things happened!" she declared.

"Our minds are made up, Nancy," Midge added. "Like it or not, you're stuck with us."

Nancy grinned. "I like it," she said, giving Cherry's hand a little squeeze.

"I have an announcement to make, too, girls," Lana said. "I have decided to officially leave the Church. Gertie's going to move here and we're going to turn this place into a women's retreat. No more underground stuff for us. We're all going to be up here in the sunshine.

"And next summer, we want to host a special week for any girl who wants to come vacation here," she added.

"And you could have entertainment, like music and dances!" Nancy cried, already tapping her toes in excitement.

"That's a great idea!" Lana cried. "Why, we can get started now, while you're here. You can help us plan."

Lana climbed out of her hammock. "I think I'll go help Gert with luncheon and fill her in on your great idea, Nancy."

Midge and Velma followed Lana indoors.

Nurse Marstad took Jackie by the hand. "Let's take a walk," she murmured suggestively.

"That's a great idea!" Cherry cried, jumping up to join them. But Nancy held her back.

"Why don't we go and get cleaned up," she whispered. Feeling rather rumpled, Cherry happily agreed, and the pair walked hand-in-hand back to their room.

CHAPTER 25

A Strange Dream?

Cherry yawned and buried her head deeper in the lavender-scented pillowcase. "What a strange dream I had last night," she thought, opening her blurry eyes and taking in the warm sunny room. It took her a few minutes to realize she wasn't in her little room in the nurses' dorm of Seattle General Hospital, and that last night had been no dream!

She pulled the starched white sheet over her head. "Yesterday I broke my nursing vow and killed a man," she said, wondering if perhaps she should find a new profession.

"Huh? What did you say, Cherry?" Nancy murmured, half asleep herself.

Nancy had slept straight through the night. After the body had been removed, everyone agreed they would tell Nancy about the priest's death in the morning. "That girl doesn't need any more shocks," Aunt Gert had said firmly.

Cherry quickly filled her in on the incident, leaving out the gory details.

"Golly, you're brave!" Nancy exclaimed, tears welling up in her eyes. She hugged Cherry. "Next time, just wake me. It must have been terrible for you," she scolded. Cherry smiled. How like Nancy to put the needs of others first!

Cherry kissed her chum good morning. Suddenly, everything seemed all right again.

Nancy jumped out of bed. "I feel better than I have in ages!" she cried. She giggled when she caught a glimpse of herself in the vanity mirror. "I have bed-head," she laughed, patting her unruly titian hair into place.

Lauren burst into the room, dressed in her old familiar overalls, which had been freshly washed and mended. Behind her was Aunt Gert, with a sheepish grin on her face and a pot of coffee in her hands.

"I told her to knock," she said in an exasperated tone of

THE CASE OF THE NOT-SO-NICE NURSE

voice. "I hope we didn't disturb you girls. It's just that it's almost noon and we hadn't heard a peep out of this room."

"Yeah, we've been up for hours scrubbing blood off the study rug," Lauren grinned.

Aunt Gert just rolled her eyes. "I've done my best with her," she chuckled. "God knows!"

While Nancy and Cherry had their coffee, Aunt Gert filled them in on that morning's activities. After breakfast, the group had explored the convent for a while and then taken up residence on the hammocks and swings dotting the lush lawn in front of the convent.

"I called Lauren's babysitter. Turns out she's the same Marge Rutherford I used to bowl with every Tuesday night. She's a swell gal. She's coming up at suppertime for a visit." She turned to Lauren. "She was awfully worried about you, Lauren, but she won't tell your parents if you promise to behave the rest of the week."

Lauren grinned. "I guess Miss Rutherford's a good egg after all," she said.

"And Midge has already found a new pet to add to her zoo," Gert reported.

"Yeah, there's kittens all over the place," Lauren said, pulling a tiny black kitten with bright green eyes out of her overalls. "I'm going to call this one Muffy."

"Kittens?" Nancy cried. "Oh, may I have one? I mean, when I return from River Depths and finally settle down? Oh, may I Aunt Gert?" she asked shyly.

Aunt Gert nodded. "There are plenty of kittens," she declared. "Pick one out now, and we'll keep her until you return. Hurry and get dressed now, girls," she said, gathering the coffee cups and shooing Lauren out of the room.

Cherry grinned and hopped out of bed. The gloom of last night had disappeared in the warm glow of the sun-filled room.

She took a quick bath and ran a comb through her unruly curls. A quick brush of powder and a smidge of pink lipstick completed her morning toilette. She noticed that Aunt Gert, who was the very same size as her look-alike niece, had left a selection of outfits for them. She slipped into a simple summer dress, while Nancy selected a simple skirt and a darling green blouse that contrasted prettily with her golden-red hair.

"I'll be back in uniform soon enough," Cherry thought,

surveying her casual outfit in the mirror. Golly, had it only been a few days since she had been wearing her starched nurse's whites? It seemed like a whole other lifetime, now!

"What's that serious look, Cherry?" Nancy asked earnestly. "Are you homesick for Seattle General? Golly, I hope we can spend some time together before I leave for River Depths. It's not every day I meet someone like you." Her cheeks were bright red.

"I'm not homesick," Cherry cried, hugging Nancy. "Meeting you has been the most exciting thing that has ever happened to me! It's just that these last few days have been the most wonderful *and* the most horrible of my life. Golly, it's all so confusing."

"Life is never like it is in books, is it?" Nancy laughed.

Lauren was back, this time with a baseball glove in one hand and an impatient look on her freckled face. "Sister Maureen MacMannish, the P.E. nun, has gotten together a softball game," she explained. "You've been voted right fielder for Aunt Gert's team, Cherry!" she cried, tossing Cherry the glove.

"And, Nancy, I hope you can pitch as well as you capture criminals because you're on my team."

Before Cherry could protest—after all, she wasn't even sure what a right fielder was—Lauren grabbed her and Nancy pulled them outdoors.

"Play ball!" Aunt Gert cried. After some instructions from Midge, Cherry took her position in the outfield. To her surprise, she was more athletic than she thought and found the game entertaining.

After two hours, though, she begged for mercy. "Everything hurts," she cried, collapsing on a nearby hammock. Nancy joined her, while Midge and Velma plopped down on the soft grass nearby.

Lauren scowled at her teammates. "You are all a bunch of sissy-girls!" she scolded.

Aunt Gert laughed and clapped a hand over the girl's mouth. "Lauren, we've got a lot to do before supper, and since you've got so much energy, you can help me!" She dragged a protesting Lauren toward the kitchen.

A scowling Lauren returned a few minutes later carrying a pitcher of pink lemonade and a plate of sugar cookies. While Cherry poured glasses of the refreshing beverage for everyone, Jackie outlined a plan she had formulated during the night.

CHAPTER 26

"Cherry, Come Quick!"

Once in the room, Cherry checked her lipstick in the vanity mirror. She noticed how flushed her face was. Was it the afternoon sun, or her heart—suddenly beating at a frantic pace?

Nancy jumped on the bed and patted the spot next to her. Cherry sipped from the cool glass of lemonade she had brought with her, and shyly made her way over to the bed.

"My, it's warm in here!" she exclaimed. Nancy giggled and put her arm around Cherry's waist.

Suddenly, the door burst open. It was Lauren, with a kitten in her hand. "I picked out a kitten for you, I hope that's okay!" she cried, handing a honey-colored kitten with green eyes to the young sleuth.

Nancy took the tiny animal and laid her in her lap. The kitten curled up into a ball and promptly fell asleep. "Thank you, Lauren," she said. "This is the cutest kitten I've ever seen."

A moment later Midge appeared. Without a word, she grabbed Lauren by the overalls and marched her out of the room. She shut the door firmly, and locked it.

"We're locked in," Cherry giggled.

"I couldn't think of a nicer thing," Nancy grinned. She put the sleeping kitten on a nearby chair. "Now, where were we?" she asked dreamily, running her hands through Cherry's short curly hair.

"Golly," Cherry gulped. She was feeling the most curious sensation; her face was flushed, but it wasn't from embarrassment. It was something else—a funny feeling that started in the pit of her stomach and worked its way down.

She didn't know quite how it happened, but somehow, suddenly, her hands were everywhere—tangled in Nancy's soft hair, touching the creamy-soft skin at the base of her neck, unbuttoning her blouse to reveal the lacy pink bra underneath.

"Golly," she murmured again, as she gently kissed the spot where the lace met flesh. She slipped the silky straps down Nancy's strong shoulders, and used her tongue to caress the delicate flesh that was revealed.

Nancy suddenly grew quiet. "It's awfully bright in here," she said shyly. Nancy jumped up and closed the blinds, leaving the room in warm darkness. She slipped off her shoes and lay back on the bed. She pulled Cherry to her. "That's better," she said softly, running her hands up and down Cherry's body.

The darkness made Nancy bold. "You know what I'd really like to do?" she whispered breathlessly in Cherry's ear. "I'd really like to..."

A sudden knock at the door startled them both. It was Aunt Gert. And she was terribly upset!

"Cherry, your mother's on the phone. She says something terrible has happened. Oh, Cherry, come quick!" They heard a key in the lock, and the door swung open.

Cherry jumped off the bed, hastily smoothing her dress. "I'll be right back," she said to Nancy. "Mother's probably lost her Brown Betty recipe again. She always gets terribly upset when that happens," she explained.

Nancy lay back languidly on the bed. "Hurry back," she whispered.

On the way out the door Cherry glanced in the vanity mirror and noticed her lipstick was smudged. "Oh, never mind," she thought, running a hand through her unruly curls.

She hurried down the corridor to Lana's office. Aunt Gert handed her the phone. Cherry could see by the worry in her eyes that bad news awaited her.

Cherry took a deep breath before picking up the phone. "Whatever the news," she thought, "I must be strong." The voice of a calm, cool nurse greeted her mother's anxious one.

"Your father's broken his arm," Mrs. Aimless cried hysterically. "He can't do anything for himself, and I can't possibly care for him and this big house all by myself. Oh, Cherry, you must come home!"

CHAPTER 27

The Call to Duty

Cherry sighed and turned on the car's windshield wipers. The threatening gray sky had finally made good on its promise of rain. She remembered that it had been raining the night Lana was kidnapped. "Fine ending to an exciting adventure," she sighed.

If only Mr. Aimless hadn't been injured in a fall, Cherry would be enjoying her vacation with her newfound friends, instead of driving through torrential rain on the way to Idaho.

"If only Father wasn't hurt!" she cried aloud, instantly regretting her outburst. After all, she was a nurse, and wasn't it her duty to bring comfort to the injured and sick? And hadn't her mother been hysterical, insisting that no one could care for Father like Cherry?

For the first time ever, Cherry wished she hadn't become a nurse! But then she put her own needs aside and concentrated on the task ahead.

"Your father's break is pretty bad, Cherry. He fractured his arm in three places. He'll need lots of care, and you are the best nurse in all of Pleasantville!"

Her heart swelled with pride as she recalled her mother's words. But it wasn't enough to erase the grief that also filled her heart. Her departure had come at the worst possible time!

Her mother had begged her to come home as soon as possible, and what with the flurry that followed, she hadn't had time for a proper good-bye to Nancy. The fact that they had exchanged promises to see each other soon just somehow wasn't enough!

A tear trickled down her cheek. By now her chums were sitting down to a scrumptious supper, while she nibbled on an egg salad sandwich, thoughtfully prepared for her by Sister Honey. She fished in her purse for a clean hankie, but found none. All she had to wipe her tears on was her shirt sleeve!

She knew her mother would be dismayed to see her dressed so casually, and her father hated to see girls wearing slacks. "Maybe he'll be in too much pain to notice," she thought hopefully.

She mentally re-hashed the frantic conversation she had had with her usually unflappable mother.

"I just don't know where to turn!" Mrs. Aimless had cried, explaining the unlucky turn of events that had thrown the Aimless household into such a tizzy.

"Your father and I were in the back yard working on this year's float for the Founder's Day Parade. Oh, Cherry, it's so darling; wait until you see it. It looks like our house, only smaller. Anyway, I went into the kitchen for some lemonade and coffee cake and I heard the most awful crash! Your father tripped over Snowball while going down the basement stairs. Oh, Cherry, I was so startled I dropped my favorite cake platter—the one Grandma Aimless gave me for my birthday last summer, with the little cherries painted on the base—and when I ran outside, your father was lying very still. Goodness, I almost fainted!"

"Breathe, Mother," Cherry said gently, fearing her mother was about to faint. After a brief pause, Mrs. Aimless continued.

"Thankfully the paper boy was just coming up the block and he went and got Doctor Joe. Your father's stuck in bed, and I still have to finish the float and make my famous Brown Betty for the country fair—and that's in five days. I can't possibly do all this work alone. Oh, Cherry, you always know what to do. Please come home as soon as possible!"

Cherry turned off the highway and onto the Pleasantville exit. It had finally stopped raining. A few more minutes, and she would be home.

She arrived at the Aimless house just as two handsome young men were getting out of a taxi. It was her beloved twin Charley and his chum Johnny!

Suddenly, Cherry felt much gayer!

She hopped out of her car, ran to the boys and gave each a big hug. "Golly, it's good to see you both!" she cried. "Mother didn't tell me you were coming."

"Mother called after she spoke to you," Charley explained, his brown eyes dancing with delight. "I couldn't pass up a chance to see my favorite sister!"

"I'm your only sister," Cherry laughingly reminded him.

"But you're still my favorite," the handsome lad grinned. He took a manly set of leather luggage from the trunk of the cab and gave the driver a generous tip.

"Besides, since Johnny and I are decorators, we'll have that parade float finished in no time at all."

"We want to hear all about San Francisco," Johnny cut in.

"I've got so much to tell you!" Cherry cried, aching to tell someone about her adventures.

But before she could, they heard a shriek from the house. It was Mrs. Aimless, and she had spied Cherry's new hair-do!

Mrs. Aimless ran out the front door and stepped gingerly through the wet grass, taking care not to muddy her summer sandals. She was dressed in a charming summer shirtwaist, a checkered apron tied with a neat bow around her slender waist.

"You've cut off all your hair!" Mrs. Aimless wailed when she reached Cherry. "And Charley, you're here. I'm so glad to see you!" she cried.

"And Johnny, you're here too. What a surprise!" Mrs. Aimless cried upon spying Charley's chum. "I'm afraid the house is really in no shape for company," she worried aloud. "I haven't had time to touch the guest bedroom and there are no fresh guest towels."

Charley interrupted his mother with a big hug. "Now, Mother, there's nothing to worry about. Why, Johnny can sleep with me in my old bedroom."

Mrs. Aimless threw up her hands. "That would be such a relief!" she exclaimed. "Your father has been assembling paper poppies for his float in the guest room. There are hundreds of them in there! Oh, kids, there's so much work to be done!

We've simply got to finish the float. Why, your father's reputation depends on it!"

Cherry explained to Johnny that the Aimless Realty float had been chosen to lead the parade.

"It's quite an honor here in Pleasantville," Mrs. Aimless chimed in. "Your father had been looking forward to it all year. And now this had to happen!" She took a clean hankie from the pocket of her apron and dabbed at her eyes.

Johnny and Charley filled her in on their plans to finish the float, and a big smile of relief crossed Mrs. Aimless's face. "Oh, I have the best children in the whole world!" she cried, hugging Cherry and Charley, and Johnny, too.

A bell rang out. "That's your father," Mrs. Aimless chuckled. "I got him a bell so he could ring when he wants something."

Nurse Cherry Aimless swung into action. "I'll just get the medical bag from my car and get started on this case," she declared.

"Your father is in a great deal of pain," Mrs. Aimless cautioned. "So don't be hurt if he's a little cross with you. Why, he was so grumpy earlier, he threw his lunch at me.

"And, Cherry, I found an old uniform from when you were a visiting nurse for Doctor Joe; you'd better put it on. There's no telling what your father will say when he sees you in slacks. And, if I were you, I'd put a cap over that haircut!"

Johnny winked at Cherry behind Mrs. Aimless' back. "I love your new look," he whispered. "Even if your mother doesn't."

Cherry grinned. Leave it to Johnny to say just the right thing! Johnny was always the first to compliment her on a new outfit or hair-do.

She gave him another hug. "You're just like the sister I never had!" she exclaimed.

"Cherry, your father's ringing!" Mrs. Aimless cried, exhaustion creeping into her voice. Cherry hurried inside. There would be time enough for talking later, but right now, she had a job to do!

CHAPTER 28

A Gay Day

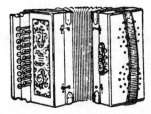

"Golly, I'm tired!" Cherry complained in a good-natured way. She plopped onto the porch swing next to her mother and wriggled out of her summer sandals. She had just taken a walk to Tilly's Drugstore to pick up some magazines for her father, and the walk into town had wiped her out.

She looked cheery in her lemon-yellow summer shift, but she felt anything but!

"Father is so demanding! Why, he's like a child!" she complained to her mother.

Mrs. Aimless just chuckled and cast another row of her knitting. "Your father can be an awful crab apple, that's for sure!" she laughed. "Imagine the fuss he'd kick up if he got a monthly visitor like we do. Why, we'd never hear the end of it!"

Cherry felt her face grow warm. Why, her mother had never spoken this intimately to her before! Mrs. Aimless passed her daughter a cool glass of iced tea.

"Drink up, Cherry. You look peaked."

Cherry drank thirstily of the tasty mint tea. The last week had been exhausting. Besides caring for Mr. Aimless, there were meals to get and beds to make. Thank goodness Charley and Johnny had taken full charge of the float. They were secreted out in the garage and refused to allow Cherry or Mrs. Aimless anywhere near there until the day of the unveiling!

All they would say was that it was going to be the talk of the town!

Johnny and Charley came out of the garage, their hair full of sawdust and their jeans splattered with paint. "What are you boys doing in there?" Mrs. Aimless asked.

Johnny and Charley just smiled in that secretive way they had. "You'll just have to wait until the parade tomorrow!"

Charley grinned. They disappeared into the kitchen. Cherry could hear their shrieks of delight when they discovered the chocolate cake cooling on the windowsill.

"That Johnny is such a nice boy, Cherry. Don't you think?" Mrs. Aimless asked. But Cherry's mind was miles away.

"I think I'll take another walk, Mother," she said, suddenly wanting to be anywhere but there. But before she could slip on her sandals, her father rang.

Mrs. Aimless sighed and put down her knitting. "I'll get that, dear," she said to her exhausted daughter. "You just sit here and rest." She fished a letter from her skirt pocket. "This came for you while you were in town," she said, handing Cherry a perfumed envelope.

Cherry sniffed deeply. "Ah! White Shoulders! It must be from Nancy!"

She waited until her mother left to open the letter. Her hands shook as she held the delicate paper. She missed Nancy so! Their phone conversations, snatched between chores, hadn't been nearly enough, for Cherry longed to have Nancy with her. Nancy had begged to come, but Cherry had said no. She was afraid that the stress of more company would send her mother over the edge!

"Darling Cherry," the letter began. "Last night I had the most wonderful dream about you!"

"Here's some cake, Cherry," Charley said. He leaned over his sister's shoulder. "Hey, what's this? Have you got a secret admirer?" He playfully peeked at the letter, and blushed when he read the contents. He looked contrite. "I didn't mean to be nosy, Sis," he said. Then he grinned. "Hey, you do have an admirer! And she's not so secretive!"

"What's this?" Johnny asked. "Cherry, what have you been keeping from us?"

Cherry blushed. "I've been trying to talk to you guys all week!" she cried. "But every time I try to get you alone..."

"Cherry, I need you," her mother called.

Cherry grinned. "See what I mean?" She put the letter in her pocket and rushed up the stairs.

"Come and talk to us later in the garage!" Johnny called after her. "We'll be up late, finishing the float!"

But Cherry had no spare time that evening, for despite modern medication and patient nursing, Mr. Aimless had taken a turn for the worse. It was after midnight by the time his fever broke.

"Your father really should be in the hospital, Cherry, but he is so darn stubborn!" Doctor Joe grumbled. "He's come through the worst of it, but you'll need to look in on him every hour!" It was six a.m. by the time Mr. Aimless was truly better. "Now go and get some rest, dear," Mrs. Aimless shooed her daughter off to bed.

Cherry slept so soundly that her mother couldn't wake her, not even for the telephone call from Nancy. She awoke as if from a fog. "I know there's something special about today," she thought. "But I can't remember what it is!"

Suddenly she jumped out of bed and hastily dressed. "It's Founder's Day!" she cried. And it was already past noon! She flew down the stairs and ran into the kitchen.

"Mother! Why didn't you wake me?" she cried. "There's so much to do! The parade's in an hour! And who's taking care of Father?"

Her mother was busy making mayonnaise for her delicious potato salad. She was dressed in a festive summer shift, and her hair had been styled in a neat French twist. And, best of all, the worry lines that were threatening to become a permanent part of her face were gone!

"Relax, dear! Doctor Joe sent over a relief nurse from the hospital. And darling Johnny got up at the crack of dawn and helped me prepare all this food!" She waved toward the table, which was covered with pies and jams and loaves of home-made bread. "He's a fabulous cook! And look what he did with my hair!" she exclaimed, twirling around to show off her new coiffure.

Cherry sat down to a breakfast of grapefruit and poached eggs while her mother finished putting the food into wicker hampers. Mrs. Aimless explained that the boys had taken the float to the parade site an hour ago. "And they still wouldn't let me look at it." Mrs. Aimless checked her watch. "We've got to hurry, Cherry. The parade's set to begin in fifteen minutes!"

After a few last instructions to the relief nurse, and a quick good-bye to her father, who was sitting up in bed and look-ing better than he had all week, Cherry rushed out the door and climbed into the family car. Her mother sped down the gravel driveway and headed for town.

"Oh, it's going to be a glorious day!" Cherry cried, feeling happier than she had all week. For tomorrow she was going back to Seattle General Hospital, and then in a few short days, Nancy would join her there before beginning her trip to River Depths.

Mrs. Aimless pulled the family sedan into a parking spot in front of Tilly's Drugstore. The downtown street was festooned with colorful balloons and streamers. The whole town was going to have a gay time!

"Oh, I wish Nancy were here to see this," Cherry murmured.

"Nancy? Oh, Cherry, I forgot to tell you something," Mrs. Aimless suddenly remembered. "A girl named Nancy called while you were sleeping. She gave me a message; let's see, what was it? Oh, yes. I remember now. She said that she can't meet you in Seattle as planned, because she has to go out of town suddenly. She said she'll call you as soon as she can."

Cherry had a terrible feeling in the pit of her stomach. She wished with all her heart that she had been awake when Nancy called. She tried not to let her mother see her worry; after all, today was supposed to be a celebration. She put on her best smile, and turned her attention toward Main Street. The parade was about to begin.

The sound of the Pleasantville High School marching band grew closer, and as the parade neared, the cries from the crowd grew louder.

"Would you look at that!" a man behind Cherry exclaimed.

Cherry looked up, and gasped when she saw the Aimless Realty float! For instead of a miniature version of the Aimless house, as her father had intended, Johnny and Charley had made a giant replica of Mrs. Aimless's beloved pet poodle Gigi, complete with a wagging tail and a rhinestone collar!

"Oh, it's Gigi!" Mrs. Aimless cried with tears in her eyes. The crowd laughed gaily at the sight of the giant poodle, tinted a luscious lavender. Running alongside the float were Charley and Johnny, holding a gigantic pair of scissors. They were pretending to give Gigi a French poodle cut.

"Oh, what will your father say?" Mrs. Aimless cried, clapping her hands. "He never did like Gigi. I declare, he wasn't the least bit sad when she passed on."

On the back of the float was a little white doghouse,

surrounded by a picket fence. Green paper poppies gave the appearance of a lush lawn. The sign on the side of the float read:

Aimless Realty: No house too large...or too small!

"Oh, isn't it wonderful, Cherry?" Mrs. Aimless hugged her daughter. Cherry agreed. Leave it to Charley to make everyone laugh. The crowd applauded loudest for Charley and Johnny's float, and was Cherry ever proud when they won first prize.

Cherry managed to enjoy the picnic in the town square, especially when her mother's Brown Betty won first prize, but she begged off the afternoon square dance. She had had a nagging feeling all day, and she dearly wanted to get home so she could call Aunt Gert and find out what had happened to Nancy!

CHAPTER 29

Oh, Nancy

Suppertime had come and gone with no word from Nancy. Cherry shook her head. "Silly!" she scolded herself. "Nothing's happened!" But deep in her heart, she knew something was terribly wrong!

She moped around the house and waited for Charley, Johnny and Mrs. Aimless to return from town. Her father was fast asleep, and there was little to do in the tidy house.

She flipped through a fashion magazine, but the pretty models only reminded her of Nancy and made her feel sad. She leafed through a cooking magazine but soon found her mind wandering. She felt like flinging the magazine across the room but then came to her senses. She smoothed its thick glossy cover and put it back on the coffee table, where it belonged.

"Perhaps a cool drink will steady my nerves," she thought, going to the sunny kitchen to mix a pitcher of lemonade. She heard a car pull into the drive, and was glad that someone was finally home to distract her!

"I'll put some of these cookies on a tray and we'll have a nice chat on the front porch," Cherry thought. But the car turned out to belong to someone visiting the family next door, so Cherry sat alone on the porch, nibbling on the cookies. The phone rang, but it was only Doctor Joe, calling to check up on his patient.

Doctor Joe was his usual jovial self. "By the way, Cherry, that was some fine float in the parade today! I don't know which was better—that float or your mother's Brown Betty!" he chuckled. "You Aimlesses sure are a talented bunch!"

After the phone call, she took up her post on the front porch. Something was bound to happen. She sat on the swing awhile and watched the sun go down. Golly, it felt like the first time she had sat down in days! "If only Nancy were here to enjoy this," she sighed.

"If only..." But before she could finish, the Aimless family car pulled into the driveway! "I'm so glad you're home!" Cherry cried, running to help her mother carry in the leftover food. Suddenly, she was ravenous!

After they brought in the food, Mrs. Aimless shooed Charley and Cherry away from the kitchen. "Johnny and I are going to prepare a nice picnic supper," she said. "Now you two go away for a while!"

Charley said he had to tidy the garage, and Cherry decided to get out of her sticky dress and into something fresh. She ran a tub of water, using her mother's luxurious bubble bath. She was glad her family was home. Even if they weren't Nancy, they sure were swell!

After her bath she felt refreshed and her mood improved. She spent time selecting a pretty party dress from among the old clothes still in her closet. She hadn't taken anything fancy along with her to Seattle General, knowing there would be little time there for frivolity!

She selected a lovely taffeta frock with a dressy shirred skirt and tight-fitting bodice. To complete her outfit, she borrowed her mother's pearl drop earrings. She paid extra attention on her face, penciling in glamorous eyebrows and experimenting with a bright red lipstick.

"Not exactly a movie star, but not bad either," she grinned at her reflection in the mirror. She was so engrossed in getting dressed that at first she didn't hear her mother calling to her.

"I'll be right down, Mother!" Cherry cried, giving her hair one last pat.

Her mother called up the steps to her. "Cherry, there are some girls here to see you!"

Cherry raced to the window and gasped when she looked outside. Could it be true? There was Nancy's yellow convertible, and inside the car sat Velma and Midge and Jackie, and Lauren, too! And that darn Lauren was beeping the horn. It sounded like music to Cherry's ears!

She flew down the stairs, flung open the door and fell into Nancy's arms.

"I was so worried!" she sobbed. "I was sure something terrible had happened to you!"

A tear rolled down Nancy's cheek. "Something terrible *has* happened! Oh, Cherry, we've got to get to River Depths as soon as possible! Hannah's taken ill, and we've got to get her out of prison! You will come help us, won't you, Cherry? Please?"

"Oh, Nancy, I'll go anywhere with you," she murmured. "But I'll need my purse!" When she turned around, Johnny and Charley were behind her. And Charley had her purse in his hand!

Cherry felt all flustered. "Golly, there's so much to do; I've got to call the hospital and tell them I'm going to be a little late getting back, and Father's still sick and Mother needs me..." She stopped when she saw Nancy's face.

Nancy was here; that was all that mattered!

Nancy, her heart kept repeating, over and over again.

Nancy...Nancy...Nancy...

"I guess they'll all survive without me," she whispered. She bolted for the car. Mrs. Aimless suddenly appeared on the porch. Her fair face was flushed.

"Where's Cherry going? Oh, she's going to miss supper. What's going on?"

Charley put his arm around his Mother's waist.

"Come and sit down, Mother. Johnny and I have something to tell you!"

About the Author

"I was born in the thriving metropolis of Oshkosh, Wisconsin," writes Mabel Maney. "'I'll never forget that night,'" she recalls her mother telling her. "'We had that big lightning storm that knocked out all of Oshkosh and most of nearby Menasha. I always thought Mabel had something to do with it,'" Mabel's mother chuckled.

After her parents were lost at sea, Mabel took up residence with her Great Aunts Maude and Mavis Maney, who had as young women earned their living as bareback riders in a traveling circus before settling in the farm town of Appleton to write their memoirs, *Circus Queens*.

Mabel's life was idyllic until the arrest and conviction of Great Aunt Maude for the murder of her late husband, whose body surfaced from under Maude's wisteria bush during the summer of the Great Wisconsin Rains.

Mabel spent the next three years dividing her time between Appleton and the State Penitentiary for Women in LaFayette. After her Great Aunt Maude's release, the trio moved to Bear Lake, where Mabel attended Catholic Girls School, graduating with highest honors in Conversational Skills and Table Manners.

 Mabel Maney's installation art and hand-made books, self-published under the World O'Girls Books imprint, have earned her fellowships from the San Francisco Foundation and San Francisco State University, where she received her MFA in 1991. Her art has been exhibited in numerous galleries throughout the United States. *Artspace* wrote of the hand-made World O'Girls edition of this book: "In Maney's refigured narrative, *The Case of the Not-So-Nice Nurse*, gay heroine Cherry Ames moves unhampered through a world populated by lesbian nuns and adventuresses, even engaging in a one-nighter with Nancy Drew. Entertainment aside, by appropriating and redefining the sexual orientation and cultural limits placed upon her fictional female characters, Maney provides a powerful reminder of the exclusionary nature of the ruling (in this case, straight) culture, with its power to define specific roles and acts as 'natural' while denying or marginalizing others."

Books from Cleis Press

Lesbian Studies

Boomer: Railroad Memoirs
by Linda Niemann.
ISBN: 0-939416-55-7 12.95 paper.

*The Case of the Not-So-Nice
Nurse* by Mabel Maney.
ISBN: 0-939416-75-1 24.95 cloth;
ISBN: 0-939416-76-X 9.95 paper.

*Daughters of Darkness:
Lesbian Vampire Stories*
edited by Pam Keesey.
ISBN: 0-939416-77-8 24.95 cloth;
ISBN: 0-939416-78-6 9.95 paper.

*Different Daughters: A Book
by Mothers of Lesbians*
edited by Louise Rafkin.
ISBN: 0-939416-12-3 21.95 cloth;
ISBN: 0-939416-13-1 9.95 paper.

*Different Mothers: Sons &
Daughters of Lesbians Talk
About Their Lives*
edited by Louise Rafkin.
ISBN: 0-939416-40-9 24.95 cloth;
ISBN: 0-939416-41-7 9.95 paper.

*Hothead Paisan:
Homicidal Lesbian Terrorist*
by Diane DiMassa.
ISBN: 0-939416-73-5 12.95 paper.

A Lesbian Love Advisor
by Celeste West.
ISBN: 0-939416-27-1 24.95 cloth;
ISBN: 0-939416-26-3 9.95 paper.

*Long Way Home:
The Odyssey of a Lesbian
Mother and Her Children*
by Jeanne Jullion.
ISBN: 0-939416-05-0 8.95 paper.

*More Serious Pleasure:
Lesbian Erotic Stories
and Poetry* edited by
the Sheba Collective.
ISBN: 0-939416-48-4 24.95 cloth;
ISBN: 0-939416-47-6 9.95 paper.

*The Night Audrey's Vibrator
Spoke: A Stonewall Riots
Collection* by Andrea Natalie.
ISBN: 0-939416-64-6 8.95 paper.

*Queer and Pleasant Danger:
Writing Out My Life*
by Louise Rafkin.
ISBN: 0-939416-60-3 24.95 cloth;
ISBN: 0-939416-61-1 9.95 paper.

*Rubyfruit Mountain: A
Stonewall Riots Collection*
by Andrea Natalie.
ISBN: 0-939416-74-3 9.95 paper.

*Serious Pleasure: Lesbian
Erotic Stories and Poetry*
edited by the Sheba
Collective.
ISBN: 0-939416-46-8 24.95 cloth;
ISBN: 0-939416-45-X 9.95 paper.

Sexual Politics

*Good Sex: Real Stories from
Real People* by Julia Hutton.
ISBN: 0-939416-56-5 24.95 cloth;
ISBN: 0-939416-57-3 12.95 paper.

*Madonnarama: Essays on
Sex and Popular Culture*
edited by Lisa Frank
and Paul Smith.
ISBN: 0-939416-72-7 24.95 cloth;
ISBN: 0-939416-71-9 9.95 paper.

Sex Work: Writings by Women in the Sex Industry edited by Frédérique Delacoste and Priscilla Alexander.
ISBN: 0-939416-10-7 24.95 cloth;
ISBN: 0-939416-11-5 16.95 paper.

Susie Bright's Sexual Reality: A Virtual Sex World Reader by Susie Bright.
ISBN: 0-939416-58-1 24.95 cloth;
ISBN: 0-939416-59-X 9.95 paper.

Susie Sexpert's Lesbian Sex World by Susie Bright.
ISBN: 0-939416-34-4 24.95 cloth;
ISBN: 0-939416-35-2 9.95 paper.

Politics of Health

The Absence of the Dead Is Their Way of Appearing by Mary Winfrey Trautmann.
ISBN: 0-939416-04-2 8.95 paper.

AIDS: The Women edited by Ines Rieder and Patricia Ruppelt.
ISBN: 0-939416-20-4 24.95 cloth;
ISBN: 0-939416-21-2 9.95 paper

Don't: A Woman's Word by Elly Danica.
ISBN: 0-939416-23-9 21.95 cloth;
ISBN: 0-939416-22-0 8.95 paper

1 in 3: Women with Cancer Confront an Epidemic edited by Judith Brady.
ISBN: 0-939416-50-6 24.95 cloth;
ISBN: 0-939416-49-2 10.95 paper.

Voices in the Night: Women Speaking About Incest edited by Toni A.H. McNaron and Yarrow Morgan.
ISBN: 0-939416-02-6 9.95 paper.

With the Power of Each Breath: A Disabled Women's Anthology edited by Susan Browne, Debra Connors and Nanci Stern.
ISBN: 0-939416-09-3 24.95 cloth;
ISBN: 0-939416-06-9 10.95 paper.

Woman-Centered Pregnancy and Birth by the Federation of Feminist Women's Health Centers.
ISBN: 0-939416-03-4 11.95 paper.

Fiction

Another Love by Erzsébet Galgóczi.
ISBN: 0-939416-52-2 24.95 cloth;
ISBN: 0-939416-51-4 8.95 paper.

Cosmopolis: Urban Stories by Women edited by Ines Rieder.
ISBN: 0-939416-36-0 24.95 cloth;
ISBN: 0-939416-37-9 9.95 paper.

A Forbidden Passion by Cristina Peri Rossi.
ISBN: 0-939416-64-0 24.95 cloth;
ISBN: 0-939416-68-9 9.95 paper.

In the Garden of Dead Cars by Sybil Claiborne.
ISBN: 0-939416-65-4 24.95 cloth;
ISBN: 0-939416-66-2 9.95 paper.

Night Train To Mother by Ronit Lentin.
ISBN: 0-939416-29-8 24.95 cloth;
ISBN: 0-939416-28-X 9.95 paper.

The One You Call Sister: New Women's Fiction edited by Paula Martinac.
ISBN: 0-939416-30-1 24.95 cloth;
ISBN: 0-939416031-X 9.95 paper.

Only Lawyers Dancing by Jan McKemmish.
ISBN: 0-939416-70-0 24.95 cloth;
ISBN: 0-939416-69-7 9.95 paper.

Unholy Alliances: New Women's Fiction edited by Louise Rafkin.
ISBN: 0-939416-14-X 21.95 cloth;
ISBN: 0-939416-15-8 9.95 paper.

first time she had sat down in days! "If only Nancy were here to enjoy this," she sighed.

"If only..." But before she could finish, the Aimless family car pulled into the driveway! "I'm so glad you're home!" Cherry cried, running to help her mother carry in the leftover food. Suddenly, she was ravenous!

After they brought in the food, Mrs. Aimless shooed Charley and Cherry away from the kitchen. "Johnny and I are going to prepare a nice picnic supper," she said. "Now you two go away for a while!"

Charley said he had to tidy the garage, and Cherry decided to get out of her sticky dress and into something fresh. She ran a tub of water, using her mother's luxurious bubble bath. She was glad her family was home. Even if they weren't Nancy, they sure were swell!

After her bath she felt refreshed and her mood improved. She spent time selecting a pretty party dress from among the old clothes still in her closet. She hadn't taken anything fancy along with her to Seattle General, knowing there would be little time there for frivolity!

She selected a lovely taffeta frock with a dressy shirred skirt and tight-fitting bodice. To complete her outfit, she borrowed her mother's pearl drop earrings. She paid extra attention on her face, penciling in glamorous eyebrows and experimenting with a bright red lipstick.

"Not exactly a movie star, but not bad either," she grinned at her reflection in the mirror. She was so engrossed in getting dressed that at first she didn't hear her mother calling to her.

"I'll be right down, Mother!" Cherry cried, giving her hair one last pat.

Her mother called up the steps to her. "Cherry, there are some girls here to see you!"

Cherry raced to the window and gasped when she looked outside. Could it be true? There was Nancy's yellow convertible, and inside the car sat Velma and Midge and Jackie, and Lauren, too! And that darn Lauren was beeping the horn. It sounded like music to Cherry's ears!

She flew down the stairs, flung open the door and fell into Nancy's arms.

"I was so worried!" she sobbed. "I was sure something terrible had happened to you!"

A tear rolled down Nancy's cheek. "Something terrible *has* happened! Oh, Cherry, we've got to get to River Depths as soon as possible! Hannah's taken ill, and we've got to get her out of prison! You will come help us, won't you, Cherry? Please?"

"Oh, Nancy, I'll go anywhere with you," she murmured. "But I'll need my purse!" When she turned around, Johnny and Charley were behind her. And Charley had her purse in his hand!

Cherry felt all flustered. "Golly, there's so much to do; I've got to call the hospital and tell them I'm going to be a little late getting back, and Father's still sick and Mother needs me..." She stopped when she saw Nancy's face.

Nancy was here; that was all that mattered!

Nancy, her heart kept repeating, over and over again.

Nancy...Nancy...Nancy...

"I guess they'll all survive without me," she whispered. She bolted for the car. Mrs. Aimless suddenly appeared on the porch. Her fair face was flushed.

"Where's Cherry going? Oh, she's going to miss supper. What's going on?"

Charley put his arm around his Mother's waist.

"Come and sit down, Mother. Johnny and I have something to tell you!"

The Wall
by Marlen Haushofer.
ISBN: 0-939416-53-0 24.95 cloth;
ISBN: 0-939416-54-9 paper.

Latin America

Beyond the Border: A New Age in Latin American Women's Fiction edited by Nora Erro-Peralta and Caridad Silva-Núñez.
ISBN: 0-939416-42-5 24.95 cloth;
ISBN: 0-939416-43-3 12.95 paper.

The Little School: Tales of Disappearance and Survival in Argentina by Alicia Partnoy.
ISBN: 0-939416-08-5 21.95 cloth;
ISBN: 0-939416-07-7 9.95 paper.

Revenge of the Apple by Alicia Partnoy.
ISBN: 0-939416-62-X 24.95 cloth;
ISBN: 0-939416-63-8 8.95 paper.

You Can't Drown the Fire: Latin American Women Writing in Exile edited by Alicia Partnoy.
ISBN: 0-939416-16-6 24.95 cloth;
ISBN: 0-939416-17-4 9.95 paper.

Autobiography, Biography, Letters

Peggy Deery: An Irish Family at War by Nell McCafferty.
ISBN: 0-939416-38-7 24.95 cloth;
ISBN: 0-939416-39-5 9.95 paper.

The Shape of Red: Insider/Outsider Reflections by Ruth Hubbard and Margaret Randall.
ISBN: 0-939416-19-0 24.95 cloth;
ISBN: 0-939416-18-2 9.95 paper.

Women & Honor: Some Notes on Lying by Adrienne Rich.
ISBN: 0-939416-44-1 3.95 paper.

Animal Rights

And a Deer's Ear, Eagle's Song and Bear's Grace: Relationships Between Animals and Women edited by Theresa Corrigan and Stephanie T. Hoppe.
ISBN: 0-939416-38-7 24.95 cloth;
ISBN: 0-939416-39-5 9.95 paper.

With a Fly's Eye, Whale's Wit and Woman's Heart: Relationships Between Animals and Women edited by Theresa Corrigan and Stephanie T. Hoppe.
ISBN: 0-939416-24-7 24.95 cloth;
ISBN: 0-939416-25-5 9.95 paper.

Ordering Information

Since 1980, Cleis Press has published progressive books by women. We welcome your order and will ship your books as quickly as possible. Individual orders must be prepaid (U.S. dollars only). Please add 15% shipping. Pennsylvania residents add 6% sales tax. Mail orders to Cleis Press, P.O. Box 8933, Pittsburgh PA 15221. MasterCard and Visa orders: include account number, expiration date, and signature. Fax your credit card order to (412) 937-1567. Or, phone us Monday–Friday, 9 am–5 pm Eastern Standard Time, at (412) 937-1555.